LINKING
Shelley

CYNA KADE

ELLORA'S CAVE
ROMANTICA®
www.EllorasCave.com

An Ellora's Cave Publication

www.ellorascave.com

Linking Shelley

ISBN 9781419962967
ALL RIGHTS RESERVED.
Linking Shelley Copyright © 2009 Cyna Kade
Edited by Pamela Campbell.
Cover art by Syneca.

Electronic book publication April 2009
Trade paperback publication 2012

LINKING SHELLEY

ೲ

Author Note

ဢ

This book is purely fantasy. It does not accurately portray BDSM or true Dom/sub relationships. Please be safe, sane and consensual in your relationships.

Chapter One

ʚ৹

Looking up at ice-blue eyes and sardonic, smiling lips, Shelley struggled to move.

The man gripped her wrists in one hand, holding them tightly behind her back. His other hand stroked her face.

Shelley twisted, trying to escape but her movements only succeeded in grinding her breasts into his broad chest. He kept her close, close enough to feel his huge, bulging cock and hard muscles while his musky scent drifted deep into her lungs.

He threaded his fingers through her hair, forcing her head to still before bending and capturing her lips in a gentle kiss. He took her breath away as he increased the intensity of the kiss. His tongue invaded her mouth in a hard, warm, demanding move.

Shelley forgot why she should fight this man and gradually relaxed into his strength.

He finished the kiss by gently tugging her lower lip with his teeth, threatening but not hurting, before whispering, "Will you really deny our link? Will you really deny that you long for a man who is stronger than you? Will you really deny your own desires? You are already bound to me. Your fight is needless and futile."

Shelley felt an arrow of need. Longing and lust made her weak, eager to surrender to this powerful man. She longed to say *take me* but it came out, "Let me go!"

The man laughed. "The binding won't be denied. You can fight but you won't win. Fighting is just sexual foreplay. It makes the surrender even sweeter. Nothing is as exciting as a woman who resists when we both know she'll eventually surrender."

Shelley shook her head, desperate to deny the reality of his words. Held motionless, she lost herself in the fire heating his cold blue eyes — eyes that slowly sizzled, melting from ice chips into an inviting and seductive caldron.

His hand stroked her cheek. "Poor off-worlder — so unprepared for a Darinthian link. We are fated to be together," he stated as he bent for another kiss.

A ripple of need and desire weakened Shelley's knees until only his tight grip held her upright. His hand moved to her breast, lightly massaging it. Shelley moaned into the man's mouth and when he tweaked one of her nipples a clenching wave of release swept her back to consciousness.

Shelley startled to awareness, realizing she was alone on her kitchen floor. Sunlight poured through the window, gradually warming her.

What was happening to her? This was the third time she'd lost track of reality. Hallucination? Daydream? Definitely scary. What if it happened while she was working or driving? Whatever it was, it had left physical evidence.

She was dripping. Her cunt felt well used. Her nipples sore and her abdomen aching, as if she'd actually had sex. Incredible, delicious, deeply satisfying sex.

Why was she hallucinating about a man she wouldn't even talk to in real life? She knew the mysterious man couldn't really exist. She didn't want a man like the stranger, did she? A man who simply took what he wanted? Yet she admitted that his bold confidence called to her, making her soar with desire.

No, she told herself sternly. He was simply a fiction created by the turmoil of dealing with Davo, Marissa's father. Damn, damn all Darinthian men and damn Marissa for placing her in the position of having to deal with these Neanderthals. It was bad enough to have to talk to one without having a powerful stranger take over her mind.

Shelley dismissed her recent episodes as a product of her frustration and fear of Darinthian men. She shook her head and shoved aside her unease. She strengthened her resolve to continue hounding Davo for information about Marissa. She wouldn't be frightened off by a vision.

She moved to the comm. Time for another call. She tapped her fingers on the desk as she waited for the call to go through. Within minutes she was once again arguing with Marissa's father.

"What do you mean, I can't talk to Marissa? Where is she? What have you done with her?"

Davo sighed. The redheaded woman on his comm screen glared at him, her green eyes flashing and her shoulders rigid. She was too upset to listen to reason and she simply wouldn't take no for an answer. He'd explained Darinthian customs to this troublesome off-worlder but she hadn't given up. This was the fourth call in a week. Though he knew it was futile, he tried once more. "I am happy to see that my daughter has such a loyal friend but Marissa is still unavailable."

"You've been telling me that for a week! When will she be available?"

"And I've been telling you for a week, I have no control over Marissa's schedule. She'll be available when she and Kytar return from their trip." Frustrated by Shelley's doggedness, he reached out and cut off the connection. Arguing with her was pointless.

Leaning back in his chair, Davo frowned. Marissa had no need of rescue but Davo knew this Shelley woman would never believe him. While he empathized with her concern, she simply didn't understand Darinthian customs.

Lines creased his forehead as he wondered how to handle her before she went public with her concerns. The rest of the galaxy already thought Darinthians were barbarians. The planet didn't need more bad publicity. There was a limit to how much the galactic council would tolerate. If the council demanded word from Marissa, their watcher Talcor might have to interrupt Marissa and Kytar.

Talcor bore the responsibility of protecting the newly bonded couple for a full month. Two weeks had passed, only two to go. Usually, the position of watcher was largely ceremonial. Darinthians didn't interrupt but off-worlders might not be so gracious. No one interfered with companionship bonds, not even friends, and Talcor wouldn't be happy if the council pressured him to interfere.

Davo's forehead cleared and he chuckled. Perhaps he'd been too nice to Shelley. He had a weakness for off-worlders. He always made allowances for their ignorance. She was worried about her friend and she didn't understand that Marissa had bonded with a Darinthian male in a sacred ritual. Davo understood why she was worried and that fact hampered his handling of her. Perhaps it would be better if Talcor dealt with this problem. After all, it was his job as watcher. Besides, Talcor didn't particularly like off-worlders and he had no tolerance for independent females. Shelley must accept that Marissa was safe before she did something foolish. Talcor could and would handle her. Davo chuckled again as he reached out to place the call.

* * * * *

Shelley stifled a scream of rage. How dare he cut her off? How dare this man keep her from talking to Marissa?

Marissa might trust her father but Shelley didn't. Imagine claiming that Marissa was on a trip—a honeymoon—and there was no way to contact her. Did he think she was stupid? Shelley didn't believe Marissa had gotten married without telling her. Marissa wouldn't do that. Davo might look like the distinguished elder statesman he was but Shelley knew he was covering up something. He'd frustrated every effort Shelley had made to contact her friend.

Shelley's stomach knotted at the thought of Marissa alone and unprotected on Darinth. Marissa wasn't compliant enough to do well there. Everyone knew about the planet's customs. Women on Darinth had few rights.

10

Simple economics prevailed over the rights of females. Darinth was the primary supplier of amoulian, a necessary component for space travel. Oh, the galactic council issued warnings and forced Darinthian customs officials to get a signed release from single females traveling to the planet. But otherwise, the practice of male domination continued and the men of Darinth were free to practice their customs without restraint or interference.

Shelley knew the death of Marissa's mother had hit her hard. Marissa had felt alone in the galaxy. Friendship, no matter how good, simply couldn't replace family. Shelley remembered finding Marissa sitting on the floor of her apartment with that letter in her hand, tears streaming down her face. She'd held the letter out to Shelley. A last bequest from Marissa's mother, the letter explained that Marissa wasn't alone. Her father was alive and he was Darinthian.

Marissa hadn't decided what to do with her new knowledge when the man had called. He had lulled Marissa into a false sense of safety, telling her of half brothers and half sisters. The lure was irresistible. It was diabolical. Marissa had agreed to visit. Shelley had tried talking her out of the trip. While she understood Marissa's longing for a family, there were some things worse than being alone.

Shelley had brought up the Darinthian vids they'd rented. The vids only reinforced Shelley's opinion that Darinth was not a good planet for any single female, especially Marissa, to visit. Shelley wasn't averse to the dark side of sex but those vids were more like sadistic rapes. She'd never realized there were so many ways to hurt a female body. The women screamed in pain while the men laughed and intensified their assaults. The vids nauseated and sickened both of them. The acts reminded them of the things Marissa's stepfather had done to her mother.

Marissa had countered by handing Shelley three other vids. "Davo sent these. He said Darinthian customs are misunderstood. They surprised me…maybe you'll feel better if you watch them. Maybe their customs have been misunderstood."

Shelley had thrown the vids aside as she'd continued her argument with Marissa. *I couldn't have been blunter,* she thought as she remembered their last conversation.

"Marissa," she said, *"they'll make you a slave! How can you agree to walk into such a situation?"*

Marissa frowned down at her suitcase. Her decision made, she wasn't going to change her mind now. "My father has guaranteed my safety. They won't make me a slave."

Shelley frowned at Marissa's back. "I've talked to some men who've been to Darinth. They said they'd never seen such submissive females. They told me some of the things the men ordered women to do and that the women obeyed without question. Marissa, they whipped women and the women begged for more." Shelley shook her head, red curls flying. "You're too independent for a place like Darinth. The men there are serious about domination. Besides, if anything goes wrong, I won't be able to help you," Shelley continued her theme of warning.

Finally Marissa yelled, "Enough! That's enough! I am going. My father wants to see me and I want to see him. I want to meet the family I never knew I had. My father promised to keep me safe and I believe him. I'm going."

Marissa, always confident, had refused to listen to any more of Shelley's arguments. Marissa had taken a transport to Darinth and disappeared. It was as if her friend had stepped into a black hole when she landed on that vile planet. Shelley had talked to the transport people. She knew Marissa had arrived safely. But Marissa hadn't called when she reached the planet. And now she'd been missing for nearly three weeks and she still hadn't called.

Stymied by Davo's implacable insistence that Marissa was out of reach for another couple of weeks, Shelley bit her lip and tried to plan her next move. She wasn't used to a man denying her anything. Davo's rigidity in the face of her pleading, begging and threatening was a new experience. What did it take to move the man?

Frustrated and tired, she silently cursed herself for not doing more. Somehow, she should be able to help Marissa. But, as much as she pushed her brain, she couldn't figure out what to do next. No one but Shelley seemed concerned and she had no idea of how to help Marissa.

The next night, Shelley tried calling Davo once more. Maybe if she harassed him enough he'd give in and get Marissa for her.

The call didn't go through. Instead, a message appeared on her screen. Blinking lights said, "Please wait...transferring your call."

Her heart soared. Had Davo relented? Would Marissa answer the call?

Hoping to see Marissa, Shelley bit back a groan when the comm screen resolved enough to see the shape of a masculine face. Not another run around! Why couldn't she just talk to her friend?

As the comm screen cleared, Shelley's heart nearly stopped. She forgot her disappointment. She forgot Marissa. She forgot everything as the memory of her delusional episodes rushed back, brought to life again by the man on the screen, the man from her visions!

Dark, dangerous and hard, his shoulder-length hair so black it shimmered with blue highlights. Ice-blue eyes did nothing to warm the glacier planes of his face, nor did the half smile that curled one side of his hard mouth. Broad, muscular shoulders filled the rest of the screen.

The man who haunted her delusional episodes was real! How could that be? Had he shared her hallucinations? She cringed, hoping he hadn't. He couldn't possibly know what was in her head, could he?

Stunned by his unexpected appearance, Shelley's mouth dropped as she fixated on the deep vee of his red shirt that

13

hinted at chiseled pecs. Her hand ached to trace the opening and find out what lay beneath. He was gorgeous, the type of masculine specimen typically found on a pinup calendar. Shelley had dated a lot of men but she'd never seen such a perfect masculine specimen.

If she touched him, would he be as hard as the man in her hallucinations? Was he cold or hot? Was he like the man in her visions? Did he always know just where to touch and how much pressure to use, with never a wrong move, never a jarring note? How had he gotten into her head?

Stop! Stop being a ditz, she mentally scolded herself. Dismissing her hormonal response, shoving aside her memories, she leaned forward and nearly squeaked with annoyance as she realized the man's smile had widened. He'd definitely noticed her intent gaze. He could probably read her heated cheeks too, she thought, furious with herself for her momentary distraction. Well, he couldn't do anything across a comm connection, even if he did look dangerous.

His eyes narrowed. "Shelley?"

The deep baritone voice reverberated in her torso like a primitive drum calling to her senses. She mentally shook off the effect of his appearance and his voice. "Who are you?"

"I'm Talcor. Davo asked me to speak with you."

"I don't want to talk to you. I want to talk to Marissa."

The man's eyes turned even colder. "That's not possible. Marissa is on her honeymoon."

"I told Davo and I'll tell you. I don't believe that. She wouldn't have gotten married without telling me."

His sardonic mouth curled more. "She was a little busy at the time."

His smooth tone infuriated Shelley, as did his smirk. She glared at him, trying to ignore the heat flooding her pelvis. A stunning face and body couldn't make up for an arrogant attitude.

She took a deep breath.

He held up a hand, stopping her tirade before it started. "I am Kytar's friend, much as you are Marissa's friend. I understand your fears but they are groundless. Marissa is fine. Kytar is taking good care of her."

"Marissa doesn't need a man to take care of her!"

"No, maybe she doesn't need him but she certainly wants him."

"What?"

"Marissa wants Kytar to take care of her," he enunciated slowly, his eyes narrowed in challenge.

"I don't believe you," Shelley said.

Talcor shrugged, an elegant movement, drawing attention to his broad shoulders. "It really doesn't matter what you believe. She's far too busy to talk to you."

"She'd never be that busy!"

Talcor stared out of the screen, cold and intent, all traces of his smile gone. His luscious lips hardened into a firm line.

She could feel waves of anger from him across a comm connection.

He finally said, "You don't understand our customs."

"Yeah, that's what Davo told Marissa and now she's gone missing."

"She is not missing."

"She's missing as far as I'm concerned. I just want to speak to her, to know she's okay."

"No. Not for another two weeks."

"You're brainwashing her."

"I'm sure Kytar is doing many things to Marissa but he has no need to brainwash her. She likes Kytar's control."

"What do you mean, she likes his control? How do you know that?" Shelley looked at Talcor with horror. Had he helped kidnap Marissa?

Talcor's eyes narrowed into blue lasers. His lips thinned even more. "That is not your concern."

"I don't understand!" Shelley screamed. Her emotions always rode close to the surface and this man just infuriated her. She felt as though he were patting her on the head and treating her like a slow child at the same time that he challenged her as a female and sent the blood soaring through her veins.

Talcor eyed the redheaded spitfire. No wonder Davo had dumped this problem on him.

Her curls trembled as she argued with him and he wondered what she'd feel like squirming beneath him. Her blouse accentuated the fact that her generous breasts quivered with every motion she made, sending an arrow of need straight to his cock. He wanted to capture those shaking globes and tame them with his mouth and hands.

He felt the threads of the binding magic reaching out to him and realized Shelley was fated to be his companion. How could the link reach across the galaxy? He wanted to deny its effect but he'd bound too many women to miss the ties that were ready to snap into place. She was his if he wanted her and she had no idea what would hit her if he started the binding process. Could he do it across a comm link? He felt the drive to try, to make this woman his bound companion. "I..." he trailed off.

What was he thinking? Fighting off his lust, he berated himself. He'd seen Kytar's struggle with Marissa, including the final ritual. Maybe he should send that vid to Shelley. If she saw Marissa's grace, would she back off? More likely she'd scream that it was rape. She certainly wouldn't understand the ceremony.

Talcor didn't want the challenge of taming an off-world woman. He preferred women who'd freely admit their needs, whose needs matched his. He doubted that Shelley would care for his methods. He had to convince her to wait two weeks, to stay away from Darinth so he could ignore the link that was

16

ready to snap into place, chaining them both. "I don't care if you believe or not. What will you do? Come here looking for Marissa? I guarantee you don't want to do that."

Shelley drew in a deep breath. "No?"

"No." he stated flatly. "I'll give you fair warning. If you step foot on Darinth, you will not be safe. Your presence alone implies consent. I'm sure you know that."

"If I go to Darinth, I won't consent to anything!"

"The galactic council supports our customs. Presence implies consent. If you come here, some male will bind you. If you are very lucky," he paused, his eyes flashing like blue glaciers in bright sunlight, "I will be the one to bind you and if I bind you," he cocked an eyebrow, "I will master you and teach you obedience. I will use you in any way I wish. Do you understand?"

Shelley's breath hitched. He'd essentially just said he'd enslave her if she went to the planet. How dare he? "You're demented if you think you can just take me without my consent!"

"If you step foot on Darinth, you *have* consented. No female comes to Darinth alone. If you chose to ignore my warning, I will master you. Tell me, are your breasts real or augmented?"

"None of your business," she spit out, unable to prevent the flaming heat in her face. How dare he ask such a question?

"I would like to hold them. Do you like it when a man sucks your nipples?"

Shelley's nipples tightened with need. How could this man affect her with just words? She prided herself on her equal partnership with men. He made it very clear that they wouldn't be equals. So, why did she feel heat pooling in her belly and fire in her veins? "How dare you speak to me like this?" she hissed.

Talcor laughed, and with his mirth, his entire face changed. The crinkles around his eyes and mouth came alive, softening the hard lines. And suddenly she wanted to know what his mouth would feel like. Would it be hard and cold or soft and warm? Better yet, would his lips be hard and warm, just like his cock?

She fought off her desire to climb on top of him. What was she thinking? How could she find this hard man attractive?

"Darinthian customs are different than yours. There is no reason for you to come here. Marissa is happy. You can speak to her soon. That is all you need know," said Talcor, reaching out and cutting off the connection.

Talcor sat very still as he fought to bring his emotions under control. He longed to tame this woman, to make her his. No woman had hit him in the gut as she had. He shook his head. She was trouble and her resistance might cause him to go too far.

He knew she'd try to find her friend, and if she came to the planet, she'd be in danger. Would that stop her? No, she was too worried about Marissa. She hadn't believed his assurances or his threats. That thought caused a twinge of irritation. As if he'd lie to her. He had no reason to lie. She didn't know that though. She'd come. Sighing, he made a call to Camer, a friend at customs.

"There's a woman who might come to the planet. If she appears, I want you to hold her and call me," Talcor said.

"You claim her?" questioned Camer.

Talcor hesitated for just an instant. He really didn't want to claim the woman, he wanted to disavow her and let her suffer the consequences of her actions. But he couldn't do that to any woman, much less an off-worlder who knew nothing about Darinthian customs. "Yes, I claim her."

Camer nodded and added Shelley's name to the entrance list.

Now if Shelley appeared on the planet, Talcor would be notified. Although what he'd do with her if she showed, he had no idea. He knew what he wanted to do, he wanted her helpless in his playroom, squirming under his attention and screaming out his name as she had a violent orgasm but somehow he didn't think Shelley would think much of that idea. He smiled. Well, if she were foolish enough to come to Darinth, he could always change her mind, couldn't he?

Chapter Two

ᔕᗝ

Shelley threw her glass across the room. Splintering into hundreds of shards, the broken glass echoed Shelley's temper. How dare he just cut her off? Who did he think he was? And what gave him the right to say such things to her? She stomped around the room, infuriated by the man's condescension and even more so by her response to him.

How could she want such a bastard? But it was as if his image had seared into her brain. She hadn't been able to shake her visions. They had echoed in her head at odd moments. Just for a moment she imagined his hands holding her down, his lips crushing hers and his cock thrusting hard against her belly, just as he had in her dreams.

Why had she imagined him? Why had he filled her mind to the point that she lost track of her surroundings and surrendered herself to him? A man she'd never met but she was certain he was the man from her visions. There was no mistaking him. What did it mean? Maybe it wasn't hallucination, maybe it was a prophecy.

She shook her head. *Don't be silly. There is no such thing as prophecy.* It was just a coincidence that the man looked the same as the one in her mind. It didn't mean anything. Yet, to know that he existed was very disturbing. How could she imagine a real man she'd never seen before today?

Shivering, she sighed and shook her head. What was wrong with her? Ruthlessly she shoved his image aside. She couldn't afford to be distracted.

What should she do next? How could she help Marissa? Because no matter what Talcor and Davo said, Shelley didn't believe her friend was happy on Darinth. Both had told her to wait but she didn't think she'd survive another two weeks of worrying. Why wouldn't they just let her talk to Marissa and satisfy her need to know that her friend was safe?

Shelley frowned. She'd never thought of going to Darinth until Talcor's words had challenged her spirit of independence. Everyone knew of the galactic council's ruling. There'd certainly been enough publicity about Darinth.

Yet Talcor had seemed too emphatic. Was there another reason he didn't want her to visit? Would she be able to find Marissa and talk to her if she went to Darinth? Why didn't he want her on the planet? And how dare he threaten her? Surely there was some way she could go to the planet safely. Her mind raced and she smiled as she decided on her next move.

The next day, Shelley went to the Darinthian embassy. Much as she wanted to, she knew she couldn't just go storming on to the planet. As a woman alone, she'd be fair game for any Darinthian male and Talcor had already threatened to kidnap her and hold her prisoner. Marissa had her father's pledge of protection, yet she'd disappeared. What chance would Shelley have? Maybe the embassy would provide protection or answers of some kind.

It took Shelley hours to wade through the bureaucracy. Everyone she talked to was male. Weren't there any females in this place? She didn't see any women, just large threatening-looking men and every one of them treated her as Talcor had, as if she were a stupid child. They were so annoying. Shelley's temper threatened to explode by the time she finally reached the ambassador through a combination of determination, persistence and sheer grit.

Shelley was tall for a woman but the ambassador stood a head taller. Gray threaded through his black hair but he still looked fit. His sleeveless tunic revealed massive shoulders and arms lined with muscles. Weren't any of these guys ugly or even average?

His impassive face and flat eyes gave her pause. He didn't look at all friendly. But she'd finally reached him and she couldn't stop now. She swallowed the lump in her throat, shoving aside her misgivings.

"My friend disappeared on your planet," she started.

"Who is your friend?"

Shelley told him.

The ambassador's booming laugh startled her.

"It's not funny. She's missing."

The ambassador's laughter had descended to a chuckle as he tried to wipe the smile from his face. "Kytar's companion is not missing."

"You know her? How?"

"That's irrelevant," he said, waving a hand as if to brush off her questions. "Be assured, your friend Marissa is not missing."

"I haven't heard from her."

"Of course not. A bound couple always has a period of isolation. She's fine."

"She's missing."

"No she's not," he replied.

"Then why can't I talk to her?"

"Next month you can talk to her."

"That's not good enough. I want to talk to her now."

The ambassador frowned. "Even if I were to agree, Talcor would not let that happen."

"Don't you have more rank than Talcor?" she challenged.

"Not in this instance. Talcor is their watcher."

"Watcher? What do you mean?"

"A newly bound couple has a period of isolation so they may solidify their bonds. The watcher makes certain no one interrupts. Talcor is watcher for Marissa and Kytar."

"Bound?" Shelley asked, remembering Talcor had mentioned the word in her vision.

"Bound—our term for marriage." He held up a hand, stopping Shelley's next protest. "Kytar's companion is fine. Talcor is guarding them."

"Then he's seen her recently?"

"Not necessarily. The watcher often works outside the place of isolation."

Shelley sat back, trying to process the fact that Talcor had told her none of this. But it didn't matter. All that mattered was her need to speak to Marissa.

"Please," Shelley changed tack, "I'm worried about her. She was fragile from her mother's death and you're telling me I have to let this Kytar guy have her for two more weeks. No. I'm concerned about her and I want to talk to her."

"Surely you've talked to Talcor."

"I've talked to him. He wasn't helpful."

"He's not supposed to be helpful. His job is to protect the couple from mundane concerns while they bond. Think of it as a honeymoon. Would you really interrupt Marissa's honeymoon."

"I don't believe Marissa would marry any Darinthian," Shelley said, her red curls flying as she shook her head. "Especially without telling me."

"I can assure you that they are certainly…married. You worry needlessly. Marissa and Kytar are bound, a binding that will be long remembered in Darinthian history. She was magnificent." Notes of admiration and envy threaded through the ambassador's voice. Huskily, he said, "Kytar is a lucky man."

Shelley glared at the man. What was he talking about? Why would everyone know about this binding thing? "This binding thing doesn't sound like marriage to me."

The ambassador's eyes flattened, all trace of humor gone. "Darinthian customs are not for discussion with off-worlders. Your friend is fine. She'll speak to you as soon as the period of isolation is done. Accept the fact that she does not need your help."

Shaking off the questions tumbling through her head, Shelley decided to threaten him since neither pleading nor rational argument seemed to dent his composure. "I want to see her and if you won't get her to a comm, then I'll just have to go to the planet."

The ambassador straightened, suddenly alert. "You don't want to do that."

Shelley felt a chill go through her at his hard tone.

"You don't know our customs. If you go to Darinth without a protector, you won't be safe."

"My friend is missing. I have to help her."

He sighed. "I repeat, she's with Kytar. She doesn't need your help. If she needs help, which I sincerely doubt, that's now Kytar's responsibility."

"Can't you give me protection so I can go and talk to her?" Shelley demanded.

A heated gleam appeared in the ambassador's eyes. His gaze traveled from the top of her head to her sandaled feet. Shelley felt as though he could see through her blouse and her skirt. She squirmed in her chair, feeling as if he'd just stripped her. It wasn't a comfortable sensation. What was it with these men? Shelley enjoyed sex. She never felt uncomfortable with men yet these Darinthians seemed way out of her realm of expertise. She didn't like the fact that they made her think of sex in ways she hadn't before. Her discomfort made her even angrier. How dare he treat her as an object?

"If you won't help me, I'll just go," said Shelley.

The ambassador seemed to make an effort to bring his attention from Shelley's breasts back to her eyes. "You don't know what you ask when you request my protection. Darinthian customs are very strict. You should be grateful that I don't just accept and bind you with the claiming words. I've long wished for a true companion. I should just bind you. But I tell myself you don't know what you ask, so I won't start the binding, something you would not enjoy," he paused, eyeing her once again, his words trailing off into a murmur, "and there is something about you… I think you've already been touched. It's not finished but it has started…" his voice trailed off to a soft murmur.

Shelley had to strain to catch his next statement.

"I didn't realize the magic would reach off-world." He shook his head as if to remind himself that he wasn't alone. "I don't think you'd like Darinth very much. You are far too independent and your temper would cause problems. But I will say that if you go to the planet, you do so without my protection and if you enter our planet without protection, any man may claim you. You won't see Marissa. You won't even be able to talk to her for a while and that's only if the man who claims you allows you to talk to her. Don't be foolish. Wait a few weeks. Then you'll see that your friend neither needs nor wants your help."

"What if I bring a man with me?"

"You speak as if the man would be under your control rather than you under his."

"Well, of course," Shelley stated, unable to stop her vehement agreement.

A tiny smile turned up the corners of the ambassador's lips.

"*Would* being with a man protect me?" Shelley wanted an answer to her question.

"Maybe."

"What do you mean, maybe?"

"You'd have to be bound to the man. Only then could he prevent a Darinthian from claiming you. A stranger to our world might have difficulty doing that."

"I don't understand."

"No, you don't understand and that fact should be enough to keep you off Darinth. Our customs are ancient and respected. If you go to Darinth you won't escape them."

"But if I were accompanied by a man, I'd be protected?" Shelley persisted

The ambassador leaned back in his chair. A smile blossomed on his face but it wasn't warm, it chilled her blood. Before she could wonder about it, the ambassador said, "If you are accompanied, you will be protected."

Later that night, Shelley sank into a chair in her apartment. She replayed her day, wondering how she could have spent all day and essentially accomplished nothing. Darinthian men were much tougher than she had expected.

She sipped her wine and thought of her next move. Apparently, she'd have to go to the planet. She didn't look forward to the trip but she simply couldn't wait and she couldn't figure out what else to do. She knew she could talk Jared, her current boyfriend, into going with her. He'd protect her. Now that she had made her decision, she wanted to leave immediately. But unfortunately, Jared wouldn't be back in town until Monday. She faced a long weekend alone.

Normally, she and Marissa would find something to do to fill the empty hours. She could always go visit her family, but just as friends couldn't replace relatives, neither could relatives replace friends. She missed Marissa.

Shelley sighed and took another sip of wine. Her glance fell on the vids Marissa had given her. She grimaced but Marissa said they weren't like the others they'd viewed. If she really planned a visit to Darinth, she should watch them. At least it would kill a few hours, she decided, moving to start the vid player.

The first vid opened with a naked woman chained against a wall. A silvery steel collar circled her throat. Her arms stretched straight up and the same silvery metal fastened around her wrists, holding them tightly. On her tiptoes, more of the silvery metal held her legs spread wide.

Shelley could almost imagine being helpless like that. She'd long fantasized about being a captive—what woman hadn't? When she was younger, she'd even gone to some of the more exotic clubs that catered to alternative needs. Unfortunately, she found the men laughable, not erotic. They were all so concerned with safety—primarily their own safety from lawsuits—that by the time negotiations were done, she'd lost all desire to play games with them.

The camera moved in for a close-up of the woman's shaved pubis, revealing her glistening cunt.

Shelley squirmed a little. For a lark, she'd shaved once. The itch when her hair started growing back had been agony and she'd sworn she'd never do it again.

She took another swallow of wine and almost choked when a naked man moved into view. Controlled and graceful, he moved toward the woman. Standing within breathing distance, he towered over her. His cock thrust nearly to his waist, larger than any she'd ever seen.

Shelley's breath caught in her throat and she clenched her thighs. She wanted that cock buried deep inside. No wonder the woman was aroused.

The man reached out and gently captured the woman's breasts. Shelley could see his small movements, massaging the breasts in his strong fingers, forearms flexing with each movement. The woman's nipples filled, stretching out as if begging for a touch. But the man ignored them. He obviously knew how to arouse a woman.

Not once did he hurt the woman. Not once did he do anything other than pleasure her with soft, gentle movements. He didn't grab. He didn't rush. The man teased and caressed his helpless victim until she was squirming and begging. The woman's pleading escalated, becoming one long demand for release.

The man laughed at the woman's pleading, telling her, "Darling, we've barely started."

He tortured her by ignoring her exhortations. Repeatedly he brought her near her peak and denied her final release.

The fantasy of a strong man aroused Shelley, even though she knew she'd hate it in reality. Fantasy was good though, nothing wrong with a little fantasy. And fantasy was all it could ever be. Shelley had finally given up any hope of actually meeting her ideal fantasy man. *Besides, just because something is good in fantasy doesn't mean I'll like the reality*, she thought as a startling image of Talcor seared her brain.

Talcor was about the same size as the man in the vid and Shelley wondered, just for a moment, if Talcor was as good as this man. Then she shook her head. What was she thinking? She didn't want to play sex games with a Darinthian.

By this time, Shelley was squirming on the couch. She didn't think she could stand to watch the woman's frustration any longer when the man finally made a quick, flicking motion directly on the woman's clit. The resulting orgasm tightened every muscle in the woman's body and it seemed to go on forever.

A wave of jealously flared through Shelley. She'd never had an orgasm like that. She could barely orgasm at all. What would it be like to play with a man who actually knew what he was doing?

Jared certainly didn't. None of the men she'd ever been with had controlled their needs or particularly cared whether she was satisfied. She wanted a man who could focus on her and delay his own pleasure. She wanted to surrender to mindless pleasure and arousal like that woman had done, but that meant she'd have to give him control and that thought cooled her ardor.

She might fantasize about a man taking control but she certainly could never just give him control. Talcor might dominate her in her hallucinations but that was a far cry from reality. Fantasy was fine, but for reality she'd settle for Jared, despite his shortcomings. Making love to Jared satisfied her well enough, even if he was too kind. The one time she'd asked him to hold her wrists she'd thought he was going to have an apoplectic fit.

Shelley shuddered and ached. Too bad Jared wasn't home. Maybe they should watch these vids together. Maybe he'd learn something. But he was too kind and she knew he couldn't pull it off. She debated watching the vid again but instead moved on to the second one.

The second vid stared a naked, impressive man too. His cock rose to his waist, thick and glorious, unabashedly aroused. The man's state of undress might have been enough to make the vid arousing but it was the man's actions that riveted Shelley's attention.

This time the woman was a stunning brunette, and in this vid, the man used a crop. His strong arm slashed down again and again, each slash accompanied by a moan from the woman. Each slash left a red line on the woman's ass until it bloomed into a flowering pattern of red, pink and white.

Shelley had never fantasized about being beaten. Somehow that just seemed too extreme. But she couldn't deny the moisture dripping down her thighs. Why did this arouse her? Shelley wanted to be angry. She wanted to say the woman was a slave, an abused slave. How could that be arousing?

Despite her doubt, she could see the woman's blissful response to the pain. Clearly, the woman in the vid didn't feel that pain was bad. Eyes closed with a half smile on her face, she showed no sign of distress. The woman liked pain. That much was obvious.

It was the man's face that captured Shelley's attention. Intent on the woman, oblivious to his rock-hard cock, he focused entirely on his motions and his partner's responses. Shelley saw his concern when he finished the woman's beating. Still rock-hard, he ignored his own needs. Every line of his body spoke of love and concern, not anger. Just once, she wished she could find a man who could wait, a man who would put her needs first.

A violent longing rushed through Shelley. She wanted to be such a woman, helpless under a strong man's touch. Shelley thought she'd explode with need as she watched him tease the woman, forcing her close to the peak then pulling her back.

As the vid continued, Shelley's hand crept to her burning clit. Using a fingertip, she tapped on the erect nub and squirmed under her own ministrations as she wished she weren't alone. Her orgasm washed over her in a quick flash, too quick for deep satisfaction.

The woman in the vid was still being tortured. The man hadn't finished with her yet and Shelley wondered how any woman could stand staying on the peak for so long.

Molten heat raced through Shelley's veins in time with her heartbeat as moisture seeped from her aching pussy. And her hand, which had never left her slit, started moving again. She sighed with pleasure as her fingers delved into her soft heat, gathering moisture. She tried to hold off, to wait for the woman, but she just didn't have the patience or discipline to ignore her needs. She exploded once and then again when a screaming orgasm tightened every muscle in the woman's body.

Shelley eyed the third vid. Could she really watch another one? The idea of Darinthian sex was beginning to haunt her. Marissa was right. These vids were a far cry from rape and torture. Were the men really that caring? Talcor hadn't seemed caring on the comm.

He was scary, which was far more in line with what the galaxy believed of Darinthian sexual practices. Shelley hadn't seen anything to account for the galactic view in these vids though. The vid revealed a different side of Darinth. Granted, domination by a strong man seemed a little scary but the men really hadn't permanently damaged the women. They'd teased almost to the point of torment but never beyond. Shelley was startled to realize that imagining a caring man so in control created an erotic tension beyond anything she'd felt before.

Shelley stood up and refilled her wine glass. She eyed the third vid. She should leave it until tomorrow but she just couldn't resist its allure. The vids seemed to speak directly to her fantasies. She wanted to see the third one.

Chapter Three

ဢ

The final vid opened with a woman tied to a table, her long blonde locks flowed downward, halfway to the floor. Multiple straps crossed her extremities with one wide strap at her waist and a smaller one circling her throat. The special table had split supports for the woman's thighs. The supports angled wide, allowing a close camera shot of the woman's gapping lower lips that glistened with moisture despite the harsh-looking clamp holding her clit erect.

The camera panned over the woman slowly, as if it were a hand caressing her. Shelley saw matching clamps on the woman's nipples—nipples that were gloriously erect, just waiting for a touch.

Shelley had tried nipple clamps before. She knew that after the first bite the clamps became an erotic focus that demanded her full attention. Shelley could never forget them while they were on. But she'd never tried to clamp her clit. That looked just a little too painful, although the woman in the vid seemed to be getting off on it.

Gagged and blindfolded, this woman was obviously more helpless than the last. At least the woman in the previous vid had been able to scream out her need.

A fully dressed man entered the room, startling a gasp from Shelley. It was Talcor! There was no denying his ice-blue eyes or sardonic smile. Why was the man everywhere she looked? The visions, his position as watcher and now this!

Shelley wanted to dismiss them as just a series of coincidences. What else could it be? She couldn't deny that she was a little freaked out by them though, especially since she longed to touch him, to be the woman on the table, to surrender to him. She knew she should turn off the vid but she couldn't resist Talcor's allure even if he hadn't struck her as a porn star.

Moving with grace and control, Talcor walked to the woman's side and stood over her.

Shelley felt a twinge of regret that he wasn't naked since he was every bit as powerful as the man in the last vid.

Standing over the woman, his hand trailed along her abdomen, ignoring the clamps and the begging nipples. The woman's moan was loud, despite the gag in her mouth.

Shelley didn't like the fact that he was touching another woman despite the fact she had no claim on him. The jealousy was real, even if illogical and ridiculous. She shook it off as she imagined herself lying on the table, open and waiting for Talcor.

"Pella dear, how are you doing?" he said, reaching out to capture her breasts in his hands. Not touching the clamps, Shelley could see him slowly massaging the woman's breasts, forcing her nipples to grow despite the clamps. Shelley squirmed. That had to hurt.

Bending his head, Talcor flicked his tongue over each nipple, leaving them glistening. Reaching behind him, Talcor brought out a rope. Carefully, he pushed her breasts together and started winding the rope around them, forcing the woman's nipples to point straight up. Shelley thought she'd go insane as he spent five minutes carefully binding the woman's breasts until they were completely encased in the stark white rope with only her nipples and the clamps left showing. Standing back, Talcor cocked his head, examining his work.

Shelley stared incredulously. She hadn't realized any woman's nipples could grow so large.

Talcor reached under the table and slowly moved a slat farther outward then did the same to the other, leaving the woman's cunt gaping open, moisture dripping onto the floor. The clit clamp still in place, Talcor slid the tip of one finger into the woman's cunt. Circling her opening, he smiled. The woman's moan was loud when he removed his finger. "Patience," he said, moving his finger to her anus, a delicate, tightly closed flower. Talcor touched the rim, leaving it glistening and the woman squirming.

Standing tall, he reached over and unfastened the gag. "I want to hear you," he murmured.

The woman complied, "Please, please let me come!"

Smiling down, he trailed a finger along her cheek. She tried to capture it in her mouth. He grasped her chin, "No, not yet. Let's experiment first. Pella, it is time to breach your anus."

"Oh Master…"

Shelley shivered and she wasn't certain if it was from the word "Master" or the threat of what was coming next. She took a sip of wine and anxiously awaited Talcor's next move.

Talcor turned and opened a drawer. When he returned to the table he was holding something Shelley had never seen before. Shiny metal, it looked cold. It tapered from a tiny end to a two-inch diameter with ridges at various intervals. Shelley's heart nearly stopped when she realized he planned on inserting it into the woman's anus. He used a gel to lubricate the object. With only a tiny squeak from Pella, he inserted it past the first ridge.

Shelley took a deep breath, trying to release the clenching ache in her pelvis as she realized the ridge would hurt coming out and that Talcor had every intention of inserting the object all the way into Pella. He took his time, never forcing it, gently twirling it, all the while talking to Pella. He encouraged her to take it all. Tears escaped from beneath the blindfold.

During the process he'd brush her nipples or play with her clit and Shelley realized with horror that Talcor was confusing the woman's senses. The pain and pleasure were mingling into an inescapable need for an orgasm. When the woman tried to squirm, Talcor would place a hand on her abdomen, forcing her hips to still. When Pella's anal opening had been expanded to about an inch, Talcor stopped. "That's enough for your first time, don't you think?"

Pella moaned, "Please! Please, Master, let me come! I can't take any more."

Talcor laughed, "You'll take what I give you." Reaching up, he pulled off the nipple clamps and Pella screamed. Still bound with the ropes, it was easy for Shelley to see how red, angry and bruised the woman's nipples looked. Talcor bent and sucked both nipples into his mouth, pulling hard. Pella's mouth fell open but no sound escaped. Then he reached down and pulled off the clit clamp, quickly placing the heel of his hand on it and grinding down.

"Come now!" he demanded.

Pella screamed and Shelley could actually see the ripples in her abdomen as she came again and again. A tendril of fear mixed with aching desire as Shelley realized that Talcor hadn't done all that much, yet he'd controlled the woman and played her like a fine instrument. No banging, no quick fuck, just a relentless intensity, mixing pain and pleasure. A few movements and he'd demonstrated his power over the woman.

This was the man Shelley had to go through to find Marissa? Maybe the ambassador was right. Maybe she should just wait. She couldn't help Marissa if Talcor captured her.

Shelley watched as Talcor used a damp cloth to wipe the sweat from Pella. He removed the blindfold and the bindings. Pella blinked, her eyes glazed with satisfaction. "Did you enjoy yourself?" asked Talcor.

Pella smiled. "Oh yes."

Talcor gave Pella a hard kiss. "Good," he said, helping her off the table. Shaky on unsteady legs, she leaned into Talcor's chest. He bent and kissed the top of her head before scooping her up and carrying her out of the room while

Shelley watched and longed for a man who could and would carry her, wondering if capture would be such a bad thing.

The rest of the weekend passed in a sexual haze. The vids had certainly surprised Shelley. They hadn't been what she had expected. She lost track of how many times she watched Talcor. How had he coerced Pella's surrender in such a short time? What exactly was the trigger? What an incredibly fascinating man. Who was the real Talcor? The porn star, the watcher or the man on the comm?

She tried to figure out why the first set of vids, the Darinthian vids she'd rented, had horrified her while this set from Davo inflamed her. She decided that the second set reflected caring, if not love, while the first set just illustrated cruelty. She never thought that there might be shades of domination. She never thought that she might long for the domination demonstrated by the Darinthian vids. Would Talcor demonstrate his power if she asked? Could she ask? Could she really submit and give up control?

The vids aroused Shelley to levels she hadn't known existed. The erotic image of being pleasured by Talcor wouldn't leave her brain. She thought she'd go insane with need.

Masturbation hadn't satisfied her. Her dildo hadn't satisfied her. Oh she'd climaxed but something was missing. She'd thought of running out and buying an anal plug. She'd never had anal sex and maybe that was the key. In the end, she'd watched the vids repeatedly. She pleasured herself but she still ached with need.

Maybe she'd just been too long without a man. Jared had been gone for six weeks. She knew Jared wasn't capable of playing the games like those she'd seen on the vids but at least the sex would be comfortable.

First thing Monday morning, she called Jared and invited him for dinner that night.

Jared seemed a little startled when Shelley greeted him at the door with a passionate kiss. She shoved aside the thought that Jared was only an inch taller and not very muscular. She shoved aside the thought that he couldn't physically force her to do anything. She shoved aside the fact that Jared wouldn't play sex games, even if he could. They shared a comfortable relationship. They were friends who took care of each other's physical needs. What more could a girl ask for? Neither one of them was ready for a commitment.

Tonight though, Shelley couldn't prevent the thought that she wished Jared was just a little stronger, a little more forceful. She couldn't get the thought of the vids out of her mind as Jared returned a tender kiss. His gentle hands moved over her ass, to her breasts then to her clit in well-practiced moves. Moves that never increased in pressure. Shelley wanted him to grab her, but he maintained his mild caresses until she came. Shelley knew she couldn't tell him the orgasm left her needy.

Over dinner, Shelley brought him up to date about her search for Marissa and her plan to visit the planet. "Jared, you have to go with me. I can't set foot on the planet without a man."

"Shelley, you do not want to go to Darinth. I told you what I've heard about the planet."

Resolutely shoving aside the thought that Marissa might no longer be the only reason she wanted to go to Darinth, she said, "But because you're a male, I'd be safe from them."

"Shelley, everyone has told you Marissa is safe and just to wait. Why can't you do that? Why do you have to go to that planet?"

Shelley stood and started pacing. "I have to find her. I can't leave her alone and isolated on that planet. Marissa must be in trouble otherwise she would have called. She knows how I worry about her. I have to go. Will you go with me?"

It took another hour of argument and discussion before Jared reluctantly agreed.

Chapter Four

∞

They arrived on the planet early in the morning. A twinge of apprehension washed through Shelley when she noticed that every man in the arrival center looked as if he'd just stepped out of one of the sex vids. They all moved with confidence and a masculine ease that called to her, and if that wasn't enough to get her hormones racing, they were all muscular and tall.

Even the customs official was six inches taller than Jared. She pushed the thought out of her mind. Jared spent most of his life at a desk and he couldn't help the genetics he'd been given. It wasn't his fault he couldn't begin to compare to these men.

The customs official perused their forms and then glanced up at them. "You must wait."

"Why?" Shelley demanded, not happy about the thought of staying in a public place where all these men could continue eyeing her as though she were a tempting treat. It was a little unnerving to be the center of attention despite the fact that she was used to male admiration. But there was a big difference between being admired by one man and being the sole female in a room filled with lusty men. She just wanted to find a place where she could hide from their piercing eyes and even as that thought went through her mind, she berated herself for letting them upset her.

"Because I say so. You will wait."

Shelley looked around the stark area. The arrival center was a large room without amenities. Meant as a transit point, not a waiting place, there were no chairs, no bathrooms and no food. Shelley was tired from the trip and keen to find a resting place. She did not want to wait here.

"You will wait," the customs agent repeated.

Shelley exchanged a glance with Jared. He shrugged. "Don't see that we have much of a choice," he said.

Shelley nodded. "I suppose. Let's at least get out of the main thoroughfare." She led them to one of the walls and turned to face the room. At least the wall had her back.

Unfortunately, Jared seemed as leery of the men as she. He wasn't large enough to shield her from the speculative gleams of appraisement the Darinthian males cast her way, even if he hadn't been too nervous to stand in front of her. Instead, he moved next to her and eyed the Darinthians.

"Shelley, maybe we ought to just leave."

She shook her head. "I'm not leaving without talking to Marissa." She hesitated then said, "You can leave if you want."

"And leave you here? I'm not that much of a wimp but I really don't like the way these men are looking at you."

Shelley was the only woman in the room. She was used to men taking a second look at her but she wasn't used to confident men coldly evaluating her body as if they could see beneath her clothes and knew her every flaw. She hoped Marissa appreciated this. She watched the customs official activate a comm but she couldn't see who was on the other end.

"The woman is here," Camer, the customs official, said. "She's not alone—there's a man with her."

The wave of rage that swept through Talcor startled him. How dare she bring a man with her?

Camer continued. "She says he's accompanying her."

"She says what?"

"She says he's accompanying her. He hasn't said anything."

Talcor's mind raced. The ambassador had reported his meeting with Shelley. She was a threat to the newly bound couple and no Darinthian would let such a threat pass without notifying Talcor so he could avert any contact. The ambassador had mentioned Shelley's request for protection and the fact that she apparently believed that all she needed was a man with her. The ambassador had smiled when he'd told Talcor, "She asked for my protection."

That had startled Talcor.

"Don't worry, I refused. She's not my type. She's far too independent and contrary. I don't have any desire to tame an off-worlder. Their practices are bizarre. Besides, even binding might not control her. She is very determined. I did, however, tell her that if accompanied, she'd be safe. I didn't explain what that meant."

"Maybe you should have," Talcor had said. "Maybe that will keep her off Darinth."

The ambassador had shaken his head. "I don't think anything will deter her, especially since she's already been touched by the magic."

"What? You felt it?"

"There is a link just waiting to be activated. I assume the link is yours?"

Talcor had sighed and nodded. "Yes, she's my responsibility."

Now here she is, thought Talcor, *leaving me in the position of protecting her or abandoning her to her fate*. He knew Marissa would be upset if he let her friend face Darinth alone. He sighed. He had no choice. He'd have to bind Shelley with the first link so he could protect her...unless she really did have protection.

"Do you feel the binding?" he asked Camer. The binding had a very specific meaning on Darinth. If the man truly accompanied Shelley, if he had said the binding words to start the companionship ritual, then there was nothing Talcor could do. But what were the odds that two off-worlders knew that? Or that the man knew the binding words?

As expected, Camer shook his head. "There is no bond between the two off-worlders. She's been touched by a link, though it isn't active yet."

Talcor sighed again. It was his link Camer felt, and of course there was no bond between the off-worlders. Shelley probably thought that simply being with a man would protect her and that just wasn't true, not on Darinth. Only if the man started the common binding ritual would she be safe.

Maybe he should just tell the man what to say. Then Talcor rejected the idea as the magic roared through him, startling in its intensity. He wanted this woman. No one else would ever bind Shelley. Since she'd been foolish enough to challenge him on his homeworld it was past time to introduce her to the magic of Darinth.

"Keep them there. I'll pick them up," he told Camer.

The customs official ended the call and walked over to Shelley and Jared. "You'll be picked up soon. Please wait."

"Wait for what?" exclaimed Shelley. "This isn't exactly a pleasant area."

The customs official arched an eyebrow at her outburst, but all he said was, "You will wait. It won't be long."

Once more a Darinthian male was making her feel like a truculent child but this time she had a male with her, although all the men had ignored Jared as if he didn't exist. Shelley fumed. The room was horrid and even with Jared's presence she felt vulnerable. The feeling infuriated her but she didn't know what she could do about it. So she gritted her teeth and leaned against the wall.

They'd been waiting half an hour when she spotted Talcor talking to the customs official. As if he felt her glance, he raised his head and met her gaze. She felt it like a physical blow. Electricity arced across the width of the room and suddenly she questioned her decision to come here, remembering Talcor's threat and his clear demonstration of power in the vid. But Marissa needed her. She had to talk to her friend.

Talcor finished talking to the official and strode over to Shelley, never releasing her gaze. She felt as if a large predator had moved into her space. Shelley towered over most men but not this one. He was even taller than she'd imagined. The top of her head barely reached his shoulders. No smile touched his hard face. He moved toward her, not stopping until only a hand span separated them.

"How did I know you'd be foolish enough to come here?" Talcor queried Shelley. Not waiting for an answer, he continued. "You should have listened to my warning." Danger emanated from every line of his body.

He was too close. Shelley wanted to step back but she was already against the wall. Instead, she tilted her chin, angry with herself that she'd even thought of stepping back. She wouldn't let any man frighten her.

"I'm with a man. You can't do anything to me."

Talcor flicked a quick glance at Jared and laughed. "He has not said the binding words. You are not accompanied."

"Wait a minute," started Jared.

Talcor placed a hand on Jared's chest, stopping his forward motion. "Don't interfere," said Talcor.

Jared looked over at Shelley, as if awaiting instructions, but before she could reply, Talcor used his other hand to cup her chin and force her eyes back to him.

"I offer you the hospitality of my home. Will you accept my offer?"

Shelley frowned. She could almost feel a breathless anticipation in Talcor. What was his game? "Thanks but we'll find our own way."

"How far do you think you'll get? Look around," he said, stepping back a little and waving his hand at the men in the room.

Every gaze—every male gaze because there were only men in the room—focused on her. The atmosphere in the room grew heavy with anticipation. The thick air seemed to choke her.

Talcor stepped back in front of her, cutting off her view. "They're waiting for you to set foot outside this room."

Eyes wide, she looked up at him. "I'm with Jared. I should be safe from this harassment."

"But you're not because you don't know our customs. Now will you accept my hospitality?" He cocked his head, waiting for her answer.

She should say no. She wanted to say no but she was suddenly nervous. Could these men take her? She thought she'd be safe with Jared. Obviously, she'd been wrong. Would it be so bad to go with Talcor? At least he knew Marissa's location. If she accepted his hospitality, she could nag him to help her contact Marissa. What could it hurt? Taking a deep breath, she said, "I accept your hospitality."

Talcor's blue eyes heated and a satisfied smile creased his face as he grabbed her head with both hands. "I claim you as mine. You are my companion. I own your body. I own your mind. I own your spirit. I claim you as mine."

Shelley's gut tightened as if she'd spent hours in foreplay. Her pelvis throbbed with heat and emptiness, weakening her and sending her to her knees, her head bowed, almost touching the floor. The words felt alive, sinking deep into her bones, penetrating her very soul. Her belly tightened even more until she was just shy of the peak. She wanted to scream but couldn't seem to find the air as she waiting for the blinding orgasm she knew was close.

Just when she was certain she'd explode into pieces, she felt Talcor's hands still on her head and a sudden breeze caressed her mind.

"Breathe through the binding," said Talcor.

"Binding," yelled Jared, bending down and reaching for Shelley. "What did you do to her, you bastard?"

Talcor freed a hand to shove Jared away from Shelley, sending him skidding across the floor. "Don't touch her. No man interferes with a binding ritual."

"What..." she tried to ask what had just happened but couldn't seem to get out the words.

Talcor threaded his fingers through her mass of red curls and raised her head. Staring deeply into her eyes, he repeated, "Breathe through the binding."

Shelley felt as though an invisible hand washed through her body, easing her tension. She gasped in a breath. Unable to break Talcor's grip, she sank into his cold blue eyes as if they were still pools, cooling her heat.

"What did you just do?" she whispered.

"I started the common binding."

"What the hell is that?"

"Simple, you belong to me now."

"Like hell," she replied, temper flaring as the pressure inside eased. She tried to pull her head back.

Talcor tightened his grip. "I told you what would happen if you came to Darinth. Deny it all you want. The binding words are magic. You just felt its power. Welcome to Darinth."

Chapter Five

ဆာ

"There's no such thing as magic," protested Jared. "Besides, I'm with her. She should be safe from you," he said, standing up and starting toward them.

Two Darinthian males stepped forward and grabbed him before he reached Talcor. Jared tried to fight but he was no match for the Darinthians. They held him easily despite his squirming and struggling.

Talcor ignored him. "Your choice," Talcor murmured to Shelley. "Come peacefully or I'll let them take him away."

"He hasn't done anything wrong!"

"He broke one of our most sacred laws. He tried to interfere with a binding. Stop fighting me or he suffers."

"You bastard," Shelley whispered.

Talcor shrugged. "I've accomplished my goal. You'll come peacefully now, won't you, or shall I let him pay for your foolishness?"

"Will Jared come too?"

A flash of steel moved through Talcor's eyes. "If you stop fighting, he will be released to leave the planet."

"No. If I stop fighting, he comes with me."

"You ask for the presence of another man after I've bound you," Talcor's voice lashed Shelley. "You're in no position to bargain with me," Talcor said, tightening his fingers in Shelley's hair. "I can choose what to do with him. It is my right. I may send him off-planet. I may have him thrown in jail. I may let him come with us so he learns how a male should act." Talcor paused for a heartbeat, his eyes searching Shelley's face. "Or I may request the penalty for interference.

46

The penalty is death." He cocked an eyebrow. "Will you still fight me?" he asked, waiting for her answer.

A tendril of fear wiggled in Shelley's stomach. Jared looked like a child being held by adults. The Darinthian men were so much larger that he didn't stand a chance of escaping them. She couldn't let Jared suffer for her actions. Lord knew, he'd tried hard enough to talk her out of coming to Darinth. Her mind worked furiously. There must be some way out of this mess. "I thought I was safe if I was with Jared," she stated.

"Mere presence is not enough. You had to be accompanied to be safe and the word accompanied has a very specific meaning on Darinth. He didn't say the binding words. I did. You're mine."

"I don't belong to anyone!"

"You felt the binding. You felt its pull and you felt my control guide you back from madness. So deny it all you want, the deed is done. Should I have him executed? Right now, right here? Would you like to witness the result of your continued defiance?"

"No," she protested before she could stop. She couldn't let Jared pay for her actions. "Please don't hurt him."

Talcor didn't say anything.

Shelley knew he was waiting for her complete surrender. She felt his grip on her hair all the way to her toes and the lingering effects of what he called the binding. She wanted nothing more than to surrender to his control. She didn't understand the feeling and didn't like it. But she knew he was serious. The men holding Jared looked grim. She had to believe Talcor was telling the truth. Apparently, Jared had broken a Darinthian law.

"I...I will...I will come peacefully," she whispered, her throat tight. "Please don't hurt him."

Talcor released her hair and stroked her cheek. Helping her to her feet, he grazed her lips with his before nibbling her bottom lip, sending arrows of longing deep into her pelvis. He pulled back a little, searching her face. "You will learn not to beg mercy for another male. But for now I'll accept your plea, as long as you accept my orders. Are we clear on that?"

His implacable eyes held hers until she nodded. Then he stood and walked over to Jared, still held tightly by the two males.

Shelley leaned back against the wall, her knees too shaky to stand without support. Her legs felt as though she'd just run a marathon and she had trouble getting enough air. Her vision dimmed a little.

What had she gotten herself into? He wasn't really going to master her, was he? She had never really believed she was in danger from him. But that binding thing scared her. Even now she could feel some kind of link between them and she found it impossible to take her eyes off him, as if he were the only person in her life now.

She took a deep breath and watched Talcor walk across the room—his ass tight, a masculine glide, rhythmic and uncompromising. He said something to Jared but she couldn't hear the words. Jared shook his head. Talcor said something else. Jared's eyes widened. What was he saying to Jared?

Talcor's voice was low and tight as he told Jared, "I've bound Shelley. By the laws of Darinth, Shelley is no longer yours, if she ever was. Do you wish to leave the planet?"

"You have no right to do this."

"I have every right. Shelley was unaccompanied. You had not started the binding and neither of you realize how vulnerable that left her. Then you were foolish enough to interfere with me. I have the right to call for your death."

Jared stared at Talcor, trembling, the whites of his eyes clearly visible. Talcor wondered how his companion could bear the touch of such a weak man but he knew customs were different elsewhere. He really didn't want the man to die. His death would upset Shelley. Far better that the man accept the fact that he'd lost Shelley. "Do you wish to leave Darinth?"

"I can't just leave Shelley with you!"

"If you chose to stay, you may not touch her. If you touch her, I will punish her, not you." Talcor ignored Jared's exclamation of protest. "It is my right. If you stay, you must behave. If you promise not to touch her, you may come with us."

Jared hesitated, glanced at Shelley, and then he nodded.

Talcor exchanged a look with the men holding Jared.

"Are you certain?" asked one.

Talcor nodded. "He's no real threat."

The men grinned at Talcor's assessment and let go of Jared's arms.

Talcor turned and walked back to Shelley, Jared trailing in his wake.

Talcor reached out to clasp Shelley's hand but she yanked away. He frowned. "You promised to come peacefully. Your friend is not out of danger."

She glared at him as he grasped her hand and pulled her close. As much as she hated to admit it, only Talcor's help kept her standing.

"As my companion, you're safe. No one will hurt you, except possibly me, and I won't hurt you any more than necessary for you to learn to submit to me. You'll learn it is not a good thing to avoid my touch," he whispered into her ear, sending shivers along her spine.

Talcor held up a hand as Shelley started to protest. "Do you really wish to discuss this here?" he asked, waving a hand toward the arrival center.

Shelley looked around and noticed that every man in the place had stopped to watch the entertainment. She bit down on a sarcastic retort, too embarrassed and just a little too scared to flaunt her normal acerbic wit. These men frightened her. She felt like a rabbit facing a pack of wolves. As much as she hated to admit it, she was grateful for Talcor's protection.

"Come," Talcor said. "We'll go to my house. You too," he threw out at Jared. "Remember, you may not touch Shelley. Don't push my patience too far."

The customs official nodded to Talcor on their way out. Talcor led them to a vehicle parked at the door.

Talcor gunned the engine, lifting quickly past nearby buildings. They rose to soar far above the street but before they got too high, Shelley thought she'd seen naked women on leashes. That couldn't be right, could it? Part of her cringed at the thought of being naked in public, much less being led around by a leash. She must have been mistaken. Darinthian men were far too possessive to display women in public, weren't they? She longed to ask Talcor but the grim lines of his mouth kept her silent.

A few minutes later, Talcor pulled into a domed area. "This way," he said, leading them toward a two-story building that seemed far too large to belong to one man. Shelley wondered who else lived there and it wasn't long before she found out.

The blonde from the vid met them at the door. Diminutive and perfectly proportioned, a smile lit the woman's face. "Master," she greeted Talcor, "how may I serve you."

Master? She really called him "Master" all the time? Shelley fumed. What a poor excuse for a woman. Didn't she have any pride?

Talcor greeted the woman by trailing a finger down her cheek. Then he turned to Shelley and Jared. "This is Pella. She takes care of my needs," Talcor said.

Shelley knew what needs Pella satisfied and she fought off a flare of jealousy. She didn't want to be with Talcor. How could she possibly be jealous?

But what the hell did he need with Shelley if he still had this woman? Was he starting a harem? *Maybe he already has one,* she thought with a twinge of anger, her desire for him at war with her intellect. She shoved aside another tendril of jealousy. She didn't—she couldn't—want such a man, could she? Slavery sucked.

"Greetings," Pella said while leaning into Talcor, her body in perfect alignment, tight against his side.

"Pella, show Jared to a room and attend to his needs."

Pella's smile widened as she moved to take Jared's hand.

Shelley interrupted. "Wait a minute."

Pella turned, still smiling, her eyebrows raised.

"Jared should stay," Shelley said to Talcor.

"There is no reason for him to stay. This is between us. Isn't it?"

She wanted to protest his challenge but the thought of what he could do to Jared kept her silent. It was one thing for her to suffer for her actions. She couldn't let Jared suffer for them so she bit her lip and nodded.

Never taking his eyes from Shelley, Talcor said, "Pella, do as I say."

"Yes, Master," she said, reaching for Jared's hand.

Motioning to a door down the hallway, he said, "Jared will be safe with Pella. We need to talk."

Shelley moved into the room ahead of Talcor. Surprise lit her eyes as she saw the floor-to-ceiling bookcases. She'd never seen so many books outside a library. Few people actually used the physical objects. The multicolored book spines and dark, rich wood combined to make the huge room feel intimate. Scattered, overstuffed armchairs completed the scene.

Walking over to the huge fireplace, set back against one wall, Shelley shoved aside her feeling of being at home in this room. Instead, she stiffened her spine and turned to face Talcor.

The sardonic lift of his mouth combined with the twinkling of his eyes seemed to indicate that he knew the problem she was having. Quite frankly, she wanted him. She didn't want to talk, she didn't want to fight. She wanted to jump on him and fuck, to find out if the thick carpeting was as soft as it looked. Her pelvis ached with need. From his muscled forearms, to his tight ass, to his broad chest, everything called to her senses.

Talcor walked to the bar and poured a drink. "Do you want one?" he asked.

Shelley shook her head. The last thing she needed was impaired senses. She already felt off balance and confused.

Talcor shrugged and tossed back his drink. Moving to his desk, he leaned his hips on the edge and folded his arms across his chest. Staring intently, he said, "I am sorry. I did not think the binding would be so strong."

Shelley, prepared to fight, was startled by Talcor's apology. The last thing she'd expected from this hard, dominating man was an apology. Perhaps there was reason to hope.

She shrugged. "If you're really sorry, then let me go."

"That's not possible. It is far too late," he said, his voice so low and soft that Shelley could barely hear the words.

Her laugh bordered on hysterical. "Anything is possible."

Talcor didn't respond. He simply stared at her, his blue eyes nearly black in the soft light.

Nervous energy forced her to pace in front of the fireplace, her words spitting out, "You have to let me go. You can't force me to stay here."

Still Talcor remained silent.

"Okay I was wrong to come, is that what you want to hear? I admit it. I goofed. Now stop this game and let me go."

Only Talcor's eyes moved, following Shelley's pacing body.

Shelley, not used to having a man's full attention, especially silent attention, felt uncomfortable and being uncomfortable made her angry. She stopped her restless movement. Waiting for an answer that didn't seem as if it would ever come, she gave up and demanded, "Answer me!"

She thought for a brief instant that she saw a hint of sadness flit through his eyes before they turned hard again. Still he remained silent. In the firelight, his face had taken on an edge she hadn't noticed before—his mouth a thin line, cheekbones prominent and his eyes, nearly lost in shadow, seemed so hard.

"Talcor, let's be civilized about this. I'm an off-worlder. I have no idea what happened at the shuttle port but I suggest we ignore it. Let me go and we'll pretend this never happened. You were right, is that what you want to hear? You were right, I shouldn't have come here. But Marissa is my friend. What else could I do? Anyway, just let me go. Whatever you think happened doesn't control us. We're free to make our own decisions."

Finally speaking, Talcor replied calmly, "You are wrong. It is no longer our decision. You felt the binding. Don't deny it."

"I felt something...but so what?"

He shook his head. "I keep reminding myself that you truly do not know what has happened to us."

"Then explain it to me!"

Talcor, still leaning against the desk, seemed to debate the demand before reaching out with a hand. "Come here."

Shelley hesitated, torn by conflicting emotions. One part wanted to tell him to go to hell. Another part wanted to run to him. She'd never felt such a blinding, paralyzing conflict and wasn't quite sure how to resolve it.

As if he understood her dilemma, Talcor said, "Shelley, I can explain for hours and you won't understand. Come and hold my hand and everything will be much clearer."

She moved one foot then the other before stopping again. Talcor waited, his hand held out to her. The sadness was back in his eyes and this time Shelley could see it clearly. It was the knowledge that he felt constrained by whatever this binding thing was that gave her the courage to move forward. Frowning, she placed her hand into his much larger one. Warmth tingled from his palm, racing up her arm, comforting her in some inexplicable way.

A hint of pity shadowed his next words. "Poor off-worlder, no idea of what you've stepped into."

Shelley tried to take a step back.

"Stop!"

Shelley froze, unable to move. How had he done that? She felt her heart race as she fought his command, unable to free herself. "No," Shelley whispered as Talcor gently pulled her closer.

"I would not hurt you by mistake but I will have you," he said with an implacable stare. Talcor pulled her close until she rested between his legs. "Believe me, I'm not any more thrilled by the idea than you are," he whispered as he bent his head to nuzzle her throat. As his lips trailed along her neck, he murmured, "I am not like Kytar. I will not coddle you the way he did Marissa."

"Well, I wouldn't know anything about that, would I?" Shelley shot back defiantly, finally able to pull away from him. She backed toward the fireplace. "No one will tell me what's going on."

Talcor sighed. "What's going on is that Kytar and Marissa are, what you call, married."

"So you keep saying. I don't believe you. I want to talk to Marissa."

"When their 'honeymoon' is over you might be able to see her. Not before. In the meantime, we have our own issue to deal with. You'll soon be too busy to worry about Marissa."

"What do you mean?"

Talcor stood silent and motionless, like a rock. The anger she'd seen in the shuttle port seemed to have vanished, replaced by a patronizing, determined stare and a waiting expectation.

"Answer me! Say something!"

"We have completed the first stage of the common binding ritual. I admit, I had not expected such a strong link. I'd thought only to link to the first stage. I had no plans of going farther. We are fated to be married and I'd like to move through the rest of the ritual as soon as possible. I repeat, I'll not coddle you the way Kytar did Marissa," Talcor finally replied.

"Your arrogance is unbelievable! Married? I'm not one of your Darinthian slaves! Not like that twit who calls you Master! I have no idea what's happening here but I most certainly won't accept or agree to any kind of Darinthian ritual!"

"I warned you of the consequences of coming here. You've already consented to anything I chose to do."

Talcor's matter-of-fact tone sent a worm of fear through Shelley. His face cold and hard, sending an unmistakable message. She had no hope of escaping this man. She hadn't really expected to be under Talcor's control. She'd never met a man who exercised authority in such an easy manner, as if he'd been born to be in charge.

Maybe it was time to exercise some restraint. She knew her temper would shatter against this man like a snow globe against a stone wall. He wasn't intimidated by her anger and he certainly wasn't afraid of it. Shelley bit down her temper—it wouldn't get her anywhere with this hard man. A small sliver of anticipation wormed through Shelley. Maybe she'd finally met a man she could respect.

She tried to think of a way out of her dilemma. "I don't understand what's happening. Please, would you explain?"

She nearly exploded when Talcor laughed. Still smiling, he said, "Your understanding isn't necessary."

"Maybe not, but wouldn't my understanding make things easier for both of us?"

"I sincerely doubt that since you don't seem to really hear anything I tell you," he retorted.

"I heard, I just don't understand."

"And you won't until we finish the binding. Everything will clear after we finish. Neither of us wants this but the magic won't be denied. Enough stalling."

His patronizing tone sent her temper flying. Giving in to it, she picked up a vase and aimed it at Talcor's head. She missed because he moved faster than she believed any man could. One minute he was leaning casually against the desk, the next he'd reached her and grabbed both her wrists. Forcing her arms behind her back, he pulled her into his chest—his hard, muscular chest. Just the way he had done in her vision. She moaned and wasn't quite certain if it was from the pain in her wrists or her desire to escalate this encounter until Talcor possessed her in every way possible.

"I can see you won't listen to reason. I repeat, I am not Kytar. You are not Marissa. I'll not coddle you or put up with your senseless resistance. We will finish this now. It is time you learn just how little control you have." He kissed her hard on the mouth, pressing his erection into her pelvis. Then stepping back, he pulled her to the doorway and down the hall.

Chapter Six

ℰℭ

Pella reached out and linked her fingers with Jared's. Her hand was soft as she pulled him away from Shelley and Talcor. Jared wanted to stay with Shelley but knew Talcor wouldn't tolerate his presence. Jared and Shelley weren't monogamous but she was his friend and he was concerned for her even though he couldn't do anything about her predicament. He shook his head. It wasn't the first time Shelley's stubbornness had got her in trouble. He'd half expected to be thrown in a dungeon after his treatment at the arrival center. Pella was a pleasant surprise and even a twinge of disloyalty couldn't prevent him from admiring Pella as she led him up the stairs.

Jared watched her heart-shaped ass as it twitched while she climbed. Small, like everything else about her, he could easily cup it in his hands and they itched to be there, massaging and caressing those luscious globes. Thoughts of Shelley faded as Pella moved through his mind.

At the top of the stairs, Pella looked back at him, her brown eyes matching her smile, both warm and inviting. Jared tripped on the last step, as his cock saluted her beauty, stiffening with an ache that took his breath away. Her smile faltered just for an instant, almost as if she felt his desire. Then she pulled him along the hallway, leading him into a suite that was bigger than his entire apartment.

The main room was filled with heavy wooden furniture. The wood was dark, like mahogany, and very masculine. Jared had never seen a room that called to his senses like this. Not one frill or pastel marred the impression of a male domain.

Pella watched his face as he took in the room. "Wait until you see the bedroom," she said, tugging him toward a door on the far wall.

The massive bed took up one entire wall. It was more like a giant room than a bed since hangings could wall off the area. He noticed rings in the wall above the headboard. He wanted to ask about them but didn't dare. He knew he might not like the answer. Shelley had tried to get him to play sex games like that but the thought normally didn't excite him. A sudden vision of Pella chained to his bed caused a much different reaction.

He looked down on her blonde head and he longed to throw her across the bed and use her. Her breasts looked like a perfect fit for his mouth. He wanted to see if he was right.

He'd never realized how powerful it would make him feel to be with a small woman. Her subservient attitude called to him. Talcor had told him he couldn't touch Shelley but he'd told Pella to meet all of Jared's needs. What needs could she meet? He hoped she wasn't off limit. If she was, his life would be hell.

Her smile faded and her eyes turned an inviting mist color. Her hand fluttered first to his chest then to his face. A finger trailed his lips and his breath grew ragged. A quick movement captured her finger. He sucked it into his mouth. Soft, he'd never felt anything so soft. Exploring it with his tongue, he licked its length, his eyes narrowed, watching Pella's response.

Her cheeks flamed and her breath hitched in a wordless cry. "Say the words," whispered Pella into Jared's neck. "I want to belong to you so we can consummate our union."

"What words?"

"The binding words. Say the words."

"Pella, I want you but I don't know any words."

Pella pulled back, staring up into his eyes. "Of course you don't. I'm sorry. I just got carried away."

"Tell me," demanded Jared. He could see she was upset. He didn't understand but he wanted to take away all her worries and cares. He longed to protect her, even if he had to protect her from himself.

Jared reached out to gather her close but she stepped back, evading his embrace. She stared at him for a moment before her smile came back. "Would you like a bath?"

Jared nearly groaned. No, he'd like her, screaming beneath him, he almost retorted. What was wrong with him? He'd felt lust before but never this insane desire. He had to have her, squirming and screaming beneath him or he'd go crazy. But he couldn't just rape her. She'd stepped back. He had to respect her right to refuse. He had to let her go. He wouldn't force himself on her. *Get a grip,* he told himself.

Pella led him to the bathroom. Expecting just a shower, Jared wasn't prepared for a tub big enough to hold four people. Words left him as he imagined Pella naked with him in the tub.

Pella smiled up at him. "Let me help you undress."

Jared took a quick step back, embarrassed by his raging hard-on. It might be better if Pella left.

"Please let me serve you," she said, reaching out to cuddle his throbbing cock. Her warm hand pressed against him, inflaming him even more.

"Wait a minute. You just rejected me in the bedroom," he said, struggling to ignore her soft, relentless hand.

"Oh no, I didn't mean to reject you!" She grinned shyly. "It's just..." Her smile slipped a little. "It's just the intensity of my response startled me. We're moving too fast. There's no rush. I just wanted to slow down a little. I definitely want to satisfy you," she finished, giving him a squeeze, her smile returning before she freed him and turned to fill the tub.

Pella bent over, giving Jared a perfect view of her perfect ass as she poured some kind of lotion into the bath. A spicy scent filled the bathroom.

Much as he longed to surrender to her, if she belonged to Talcor, then doing anything with Pella could be very dangerous. "But you belong to Talcor, don't you? He's already warned me against touching Shelley."

"Has he?" A startled expression flitted across her face.

"Most emphatically. Doesn't that prohibition apply to you too?"

"Talcor told me to take care of your needs and I intend to."

"So...what? You're going to have sex with me because he told you to?" Jared's cock wilted as he spoke the words. He didn't want any woman who was just doing a job.

Pella sighed and sat on the edge of the tub. "No. That's not it at all." She frowned as she chose her next words. "It's so hard to explain. You don't know our customs but..." She paused and then smiled again. "Think of it like dating. Talcor and I were dating. We've always known we wouldn't go farther."

"You mean get married?"

"Married." She savored the word. "Yes, that's what you'd call it. Yes, we wouldn't get married. Our relationship is — was — convenient."

"Was? Is it over?"

"Maybe," said Pella slowly. "If he warned you off Shelley, then it probably is finished."

"But aren't you jealous?"

"Why? Talcor has been a good companion. He's protected me and treated me well but the magic between us simply isn't strong enough to go farther. Neither of us would be happy if we tried to complete the binding, even if the magic let us."

"Magic? Binding? I don't know what you're talking about but it sounds like you and Talcor are done and I'm a pity fuck!"

Pella spit out an expression of disgust. "I am not going to have sex with you. I will satisfy your needs but no more. I won't have sex with you without the binding. And I wouldn't even consider doing that much if I didn't want you. It has nothing to do with Talcor, nothing to do with Shelley. This is between you and me. There are no ghosts in our bed!"

"But—"

Pella interrupted him by standing and winding her hands through his hair, pulling his head down for a quick kiss. "Don't make this difficult," she murmured against his lips. "I want you. You want me. Let me take care of you—that's all that's important." Moving a hand to his crotch, she stoked his cock back to attention.

Unable to ignore the sensations flooding him, Jared reached down and cupped Pella's ass, pulling her tight. His tongue dove into her mouth and he forgot his concerns as he focused on her. She was the only important thing in his life. Nothing else mattered.

After a minute, Pella pulled back from Jared.

He reluctantly let her go, aching with need, wanting nothing more than to grab her and fuck her. Why was she playing so coy? One minute she was hotter than any woman he'd known and the next she went cold on him. When he groaned, her tinkling laugh washed over him.

"I don't understand. Are we having sex or not? Are you just teasing me?"

She grinned. "Oh, I'm not just teasing. I will satisfy you. But that's all I'll do. I'll not have sex with you."

"My cock disagrees with that statement. It's just getting harder and harder with no release in sight. I want you."

"No, we are most definitely not going to have sex right now. I will satisfy you but there's no rush. You need to learn to slow down. We have all the time we need. Do you want to continue in the bedroom or in the bath?"

"The floor's fine," retorted Jared. Reaching out and circling an arm around her waist, he pulled Pella down with him. Rolling her under him, knowing the thick carpeting cushioned her back, he pressed his throbbing cock against her pelvis. Capturing her face between his hands, he licked the corners of her mouth then gently nipped her lips before sinking his tongue deeply into her mouth.

He actually felt her sigh as she relaxed and went boneless beneath him. Her responsiveness inflamed him. Yet once again, she tried to pull away from him and he went cold as she cried, "Stop! Stop! Stop!"

"Get out then," he growled, frustrated and confused by her actions.

"Jared, you don't understand."

"Then explain because I don't want to stop," he groaned, and rolled off her.

"I don't want to stop either but we can't have sex, not yet. I'm still Talcor's companion. He can feel this!"

Talcor's name sent a chill through Jared. "What do you mean, he can feel this?"

Sighing, Pella said, "Let's get comfortable and I'll tell you what I know."

Jared frowned. "That sounds very mysterious."

"Yes, that's it exactly," Pella said, walking back into the bedroom.

Jared's frown deepened as he got up and followed her.

"Sit there." Pella pointed to an overstuffed armchair.

Jared sank into the chair. He was startled when Pella came over to him, spread his legs and knelt between them.

Lifting her chin, she asked, "Do you want release or an explanation first?"

Jared's breath caught in his throat. To have such an incredibly beautiful woman kneeling between his legs was more erotic than anything he'd ever seen before. Much as he wanted to know what was happening, he could no longer deny his needs. "I wouldn't hear or understand an explanation right now. Satisfy me first. I don't want to be teased anymore."

"Then relax back," she said, pushing against his chest. "Don't do anything, just let me pleasure you."

Jared leaned his head back as Pella unzipped his pants. He groaned when her warm, small hand freed his cock and nearly came when her moist tongue licked from the base of his cock to the tip. Hot breath played over him just an instant before she swallowed his entire cock in one quick motion. His thighs clenched, capturing her even as his hands moved to her head. Threading his fingers through her hair, he groaned.

Through the mists of arousal, he could feel her tongue and teeth laving and nipping his cock as she slowly raised and lowered her head. He fought the urge to hold her down and force her to encompass his cock again. He'd been sucked before but never like this. Pella's talented mouth seemed to feel just how long she could hold a position before he'd come and she stopped just before he'd explode, keeping him on the peak until he lost all track of time, lost in the sensations Pella created.

Finally, his hands fell from her hair, unable to maintain the concentration necessary for even that small action. His groans filled the room as he floated on a bed of need. He could feel his cock being swallowed by her throat. He'd never imagined he could go so deep into any woman's mouth. The rippling motions of her throat and the quick, sharp pressure as her hands grabbed his balls and squeezed sent him over the edge and his cum shot deep into Pella's throat.

Jared slowly came back to awareness. Pella's head still lay in his lap and with great effort he lifted a hand to touch her hair.

She took a deep breath before slowly raising her head and looking up at him. Smiling, she asked, "Was that satisfactory?"

"I've never felt anything like it."

"Of course not, we're fated to be bound."

"Bound? Okay, I believe I can think well enough to follow an explanation now."

Pella sat back on her heels, still at Jared's feet, between his legs.

Jared had never thought about the eroticism of having a submissive woman but he was beginning to see possibilities. Even though he wasn't sure he'd call Pella submissive. She seemed to be controlling every aspect of this encounter.

As if reading his mind, she said, "I know what is happening to us, you don't."

Yanking his mind away from Pella's considerable charms, Jared focused on the strangeness of her words. "What do you mean?"

"Early in our planet's history, Darinth was a very dangerous world. The wild animals and poisonous plants were the least of our problems. Our greatest problem was the lack of females. Few females lived to child-bearing age. Our population was in danger of extinction. Only if the females were protected could our species survive. Over time, Darinthian magic evolved. I imagine it is for the same reason as marriage evolved on your planet. Women—the physically weaker gender—needed protection from the dangers, not only animals and plants but protection from men as well."

"You mean the men killed women?"

"Men had needs they'd satisfy with anyone. Being physically stronger, sometimes they weren't as careful with women as they needed to be."

"You mean they raped women?"

"Yes, they raped women. Any woman, even ones too young or pregnant ones."

"I'm not sure that's changed, if galactic rumor is anything to go by."

"The galaxy knows little of current practices and what I'm about to tell you is sacred. You must promise me not to talk about it to outsiders."

"Once again, the mystery."

"Yes, it is mysterious. Promise me!"

"Okay, I promise. Somehow, I doubt anyone will believe me anyway, right?"

Pella grinned. "Now you're beginning to understand. There is magic on Darinth. The magic evolved over a number of years to protect our species and save us from destruction."

"You make it sound alive."

"Sometimes it feels alive."

"Is it a religion?"

"Sacred yes, but not a religion in your sense of the word. We honor and respect the magic—no Darinthian pits himself against it—but there is no tribute or organized following."

"Sacred but not a religion. Got it, go on. What does the binding have to do with all this?"

"There are three main stages leading to companionship."

"Companionship, like marriage?"

"Yes, you can think of it as marriage but it goes far beyond that pallid institution. Bound companions can read each other's emotions. They know what their partners are feeling. With experience, they know each others' thoughts. There is no divorce, once bound a couple is bound for life—"

Jared interrupted. "Does that mean you're bound to Talcor for life?"

"Lucky for us, no. As I said, there are three stages to the binding. The first binding, the second binding where the female receives her collar and then sex. Talcor and I are in the first binding stage. The first binding is easily broken, like dating on your world. It is a commitment but a very weak one. Unlike your world though, when the first binding takes place, a couple immediately knows how far the binding can go. As I mentioned before, Talcor and I knew the binding wouldn't progress further. That's why he and I could have sex. That's why I could pleasure you."

"I'm not sure I follow that."

"Binding and collaring must occur before sex. If they don't, then sex stops the process."

"Why?"

"No one knows. That is just the way it works. We think, since companionship was evolved to protect women that denying a man sex at the dating stage would lead to bound couples more committed to each other."

"So basically, there's magic on this planet that tells couples when they should be together. Sounds kind of Machiavellian to me. Where's the free will?"

"And has free will on your planet led to great marriages?" asked Pella with an arched eyebrow.

"I see what you mean," Jared reluctantly admitted. "But what's this magic have to do with us?"

"The strength of our connection leads me to believe we should be a bonded couple."

"You mean we'd always be together?"

"Yes. How do you feel about that?"

The thought of Pella belonging to him forever took Jared's breath away. He'd shied away from marriage and commitment, but the thought of being with Pella forever felt right and he couldn't wait for their binding to be complete. The knowledge that she was still linked to Talcor disturbed him and he hoped she'd be free soon.

He didn't care if Talcor got angry. He needed Pella. He leaned down and kissed her. "I'd like that very much. I don't believe in your magic but since you do, how do I make you my companion?"

Pella sighed and stood. "I don't know if you *can* make it happen. Marissa and Kytar proved that an off-worlder can bind with a Darinthian but you don't know the words or the rituals."

"Tell me what to do!"

"I can't! Only a man can tell you." Shaking her head, she said, "I'll have to talk to Talcor."

"Obviously that thought doesn't thrill me."

"I can do one thing for us," she said, hesitating.

"What?"

Taking a deep breath, she said, "I renounce my bonds with Talcor." Wincing, she repeated in a whisper, "I renounce my bonds with Talcor."

"What just happened?"

Pella shook her head and smiled. "We needn't worry about it right now." Smiling, she said, "Let's play."

"But I can't fuck you, right?"

"That's right." Her laugh tinkled. "There are many other forms of satisfaction besides intercourse. Wouldn't you like to explore some of them?" she asked, holding out her hand.

Jared laughed, unable to maintain his tension in the face of her joyous playfulness. He reached out and took her hand.

Chapter Seven

ॐ

Talcor felt the play of Shelley's emotions as he led her down the hallway. Fear, doubt, frustration, anger and lust—a delightful combination of warring feelings confused her intellect. Talcor doubted she knew how to handle such a mixture with anything other than anger. Her temper was fierce. If he hadn't known the source of her anger he'd have called her a virago. He did know though. Underlying all her confusion was the clear thread of longing, longing for him. A longing she wanted to deny. A longing he yearned to satisfy.

Shelley didn't realize the first stage of the binding gave him a decided advantage over any woman but especially a woman who was as naive and innocent of Darinthian customs as she. For a brief moment, he wondered if he should explain more. He definitely had an unfair advantage. He knew if he gave Shelley any opening, she'd continue her useless resistance and while he appreciated a good game of dominance, he didn't want to play it with her right now. He didn't have enough control over his emotions.

The binding process wasn't helping his focus. The magic beat at Talcor, demanding he finish the binding. He must not take the risk of losing her. He must finish making her his companion for life. While he hadn't planned on being bound to her for life, the thought was not entirely disturbing.

He shoved aside the feeling. Shelley wasn't ready to surrender just yet and he wouldn't force her compliance. He couldn't force the next step in the binding. The next step had to be voluntary, though she didn't know that.

Fighting his desire, he struggled to keep his conflicting urges under control. The urge to protect Shelley, though she was not a woman he would have willingly chosen. Sympathy for her because she really had no clue as to how little control she had of her life now. He responded to her needs and lust. She wanted him to be strong, even as she fought the need. Feeling out of control, he ruthlessly shoved aside all his emotions. The most important thing right now was to get Shelley to accept her position as his companion. The magic of the binding allowed him no other option.

Talcor fought to keep his feelings under control. She didn't understand that her defiance inflamed him, calling to his dark side. The side that really liked dominating women, pushing them to their extreme limits. It wouldn't do to play games in anger. He had to calm down and stay in control.

Unlocking the door at the end of the hallway, Talcor guided Shelley into a large room.

Shelley gasped as she realized the room matched the one she'd seen in his vid. The vid hadn't revealed that there were no windows and the silence made her certain the room was sound proofed. This is where Talcor played his games and somewhere in this room was a recording device. Shelley had no desire to star in one of Talcor's vids! She shivered despite the fire burning brightly in a central pit.

Chains hung on one wall. Another wall displayed a selection of whips, crops and floggers. Leather restraints hung down from a table on one side of the room. Shelley could see a dildo in an open drawer and other objects she didn't recognize.

A wave of longing rushed through her, weakening her knees. Talcor wouldn't negotiate like the others she'd experimented with. He'd demand and order her. He wouldn't accept her control or independence. The thought should terrify her but instead a deep ache gripped her as her nipples tightened with need.

"No," she moaned, and tried to step back. But Talcor stood behind her, stopping her motion. She felt his hard body pressed firmly to her back.

He quickly circled an arm around her waist, pulling her even closer. Holding her so tightly that she could feel his cock, hard and throbbing, as if knocking and demanding entrance. She closed her eyes, overwhelmed by the sensation of him. Energy seemed to surround them and bind them into one being.

Talcor bent his head and whispered into her ear, "This is my playroom. Would you like to play?"

His seductive baritone sent a thrumming heat through Shelley's body. She nearly moaned her assent. Instead she forced words out of her tight throat. "I've seen your vid. I've seen what you do in this room. I've seen what you did to your little twit in here. Use her! Leave me alone!"

Talcor's eyes narrowed. "Twit? You've used that word before. I don't recognize it, but if you mean Pella, I don't like your derogatory tone. She knows how to be a good companion. She longs to please me, unlike you."

Shelley paused, wondering if she'd pushed him too far, bitterly regretting saying anything, but she was too used to opening her mouth when she shouldn't. Confusion and fear made her angry. "I'll call her anything I like! She had no pride. She begged you to satisfy her."

"How do you know?"

"I saw a vid Davo sent Marissa! It was disgusting," Shelley lied. She would never admit to this man how much the vid had aroused her and how jealous she was of Pella.

"My vid…" Talcor paused before laughing. "How many times did you watch it?"

"Once was too much," Shelley lied. "I'm not your slave. I'm not like Pella. Let me go!"

"No! Your words don't match your emotions. Indeed your arousal beats at me, calling to me. I want to pleasure you until you're mindless, until you admit your needs and your feelings, until you scream my name, begging for an orgasm I'll hold just out of reach," Talcor said, sending shivers down her back.

How could his voice be so soft, so seductive when he was so hard? She wanted to scream at him. She wanted to fuck him. He'd barely touched her and she was aroused to a frenzy of longing, spiced with just a touch of fear and uncertainty. Talcor could do anything he pleased and there was no way to fight back. Jared couldn't help her, no one could. Her vision dimmed as her knees weakened and the tightness in her throat cut off her air.

"Breathe," Talcor demanded, stroking the side of her face. "Listen to my voice, follow it back and just breathe. Don't try to fight the magic. You want and need what I offer." Talcor felt Shelley's surface anger covering her more primitive needs. Shelley might give words to the lie but her emotions didn't and she felt anything but disgust at the memory of the vid.

Talcor felt his words swirling around in Shelley's head. She wasn't even trying to make sense of them, easily ignoring their meaning. She leaned back against his broad chest, letting him support her. He felt it when the sensation of safety enveloped her. The wave of dizziness that had threatened to overwhelm her receded. She held still, clearly buffeted and bewildered by the strength of her emotions. Talcor let his fingertips gently stroke her face, soothing and lulling her into peaceful acceptance at the same time that he heard the voice in her head raging against her surrender to a strange man on a strange planet.

Talcor took a deep breath in an attempt to control his lust, her momentary surrender intoxicating. Her emotions called to him. Whether she admitted it or not, she liked his demonstrations of power. Her soft body trembled in his grip. The binding had been more violent than he'd thought possible. He should let her recover but he couldn't seem to let go. *Mine,* he thought with grim satisfaction. He'd warned her of what would happen if she came to Darinth. But she'd ignored his warning.

Even better, she had responded to the sight of his toys. She might deny that she wanted a strong man but her body betrayed her. The undersides of her breasts rubbed his arm as her chest heaved with her struggle to breathe. The thought of his control aroused her and her arousal fed his.

Talcor fought his raging need. He craved absolute power over women. He loved the way a woman's body responded to pain and to pleasure, the delicate mix creating an irresistible need that no woman he'd been with had ever been able to fight.

At some point Shelley would surrender to his control. He'd make sure she had no choice.

Absolute power combined with a woman's helplessness called to his senses and he loved the fight to stay focused on the woman's needs, confusing her senses while holding her on the cusp, not crossing the point where pain just hurt. Not too much pleasure, not too much pain, just continually blurring her senses until she overloaded and begged for the release only he could grant.

Power combined with responsibility. He'd never damaged any of his playmates and he wouldn't damage Shelley. He cherished his women, even when they didn't realize how far they could go. Given Shelley's response to his toys, he wondered just how far *she* could go. He had to find out. He wouldn't make Kytar's mistake—he wouldn't give her a choice.

Stunned by the power of the connection they'd formed, he fought the urge to slam her to the floor and simply take her. What would happen when he finalized the binding? Is this what Kytar felt? If so, no wonder Kytar had asked for a watcher. How had Kytar made it through the rituals without attacking Marissa?

Kytar had told him of its power but Talcor hadn't believed any link could be so strong. He'd linked many other women, including Pella, but none had responded like Shelley. None had generated the clawing need he felt deep in his gut like an ache that only she could relieve. He didn't want to take her farther. He didn't want to honor an off-worlder by collaring her. But the binding worked both ways and right at this moment he was trapped by it every bit as much as she was. He'd never felt this kind of link and he wished he didn't feel it with her. The magic left him no choice. She belonged to him. He had to make sure she could never leave Darinth.

Taming Shelley would challenge all his considerable control. But he knew he couldn't deny the magic of the binding. He looked down on her fiery hair. He felt her fury and her fear and yes, her lust. She had no understanding of Darinthian customs. He reminded himself that, despite her temper and apparent independence, she was far more vulnerable than she believed. A surge of protectiveness took the edge off Talcor's lust. He couldn't push her too fast or too far. And even though her neck looked bare and he longed to see his collar marking her, he knew he needed to be patient. He would gain her acceptance but he couldn't rush her.

Focused on Shelley, Talcor was unprepared for the roaring wave of happiness and excitement that slammed into him. Momentarily disoriented, he thought Shelley had decided to accept him, to accept their binding. Then, with a twinge of disappointment, he realized it wasn't Shelley's emotions he was feeling.

It had been years since he'd been linked to two women. He'd forgotten the turmoil they could cause. Linked to both Shelley and Pella, it took him a moment to separate their emotions. Shelley was still angry, confused and fearful. Pella though, Pella was ecstatically happy. In the past, he'd felt her joy but he'd never felt such clear and ringing happiness. He probed deeper and Pella's emotions raged through him like a blinding shard. Lust, frustration and anxiety mixed in a potent blend and he realized she'd found her mate...in Jared?

Jared, that weak, sniveling off-world man? How was that possible? Jared had no understanding of the binding. He couldn't bind Pella. Yet, Talcor couldn't deny Pella's unmistakable response to the man. Like a blow to his heart, he felt Pella crack their bond. It wasn't broken yet. A total break required a response from Talcor, one he wasn't quite ready to give.

Talcor stood stunned, momentarily forgetting Shelley. He'd known he'd have to free Pella to finish the bond with Shelley but he hadn't expected it to be like this, with an off-worlder. He wasn't convinced that Pella would be safe with the man. It was a timely reminder though that he wasn't quite free to finish the binding with Shelley.

First, he needed to free Pella and she'd taken the first step. Always trying to please him, he'd determine later if she really felt bound with Jared or just knew he needed to be free.

In the meantime though, it reminded him that he couldn't collar Shelley tonight, as much as he wished to. He could however give her a taste of what awaited her as his companion and he could gain her agreement to accept his collar. Everything else could be settled tomorrow.

"Ouch." Shelley squirmed against his arm, which had unconsciously tightened as Talcor sorted Pella's emotions. Shelley's exclamation reminded him that he had a more immediate problem.

Shoving aside any thought of Pella, Talcor focused on the squirming woman in his arms.

"I will have your consent to the final stage tonight. I am sorry you are not ready but you were warned."

One hand rested lightly on her head, pushing gently, tipping her head and exposing her throat. His lips were soft as he nibbled on her ear but they hardened as he trailed kisses down her neck. Shivers ran down her back, straight to her pelvis, inflaming the heat she already felt. Her pussy burned for this man. Somehow, as much as she wanted to deny it, she knew that only Talcor could put out the fire he had started.

His kisses stopped at the juncture of her neck and shoulder. She felt the pulling suck of his mouth as he marked her. It took every ounce of Shelley's self-control not to scream for more. She briefly went boneless, leaning back against his strength, ready to promise anything if only he'd continue his assault.

Startled by her thoughts, she raised a hand to push him away. This was too dangerous.

He captured her wrist and pressed her hand against his hair. Her fingers curled as she felt the soft warmth of his blue-black hair. Still holding her wrist, he turned his head and kissed the pulse point, sending even more heat surging into her veins. She gasped as her pussy dripped with moisture and tightened with need.

She longed to yell at him. At the same time, she couldn't deny her attraction. She'd never encountered a man who simply ignored her wishes. She was his prisoner. Though her mind screamed foul, her body responded to his strength.

He kissed her temple and tilted her head the other way. She moaned as he repeated his actions on the other side. The sucking kiss sent arcs of need deep inside. Her entire body clenched in fevered pleasure. The material of her bra chaffed the tender, tight buds of her nipples. She wanted his clever mouth on her breasts. Her clit throbbed for a caress. Her pussy had never felt so empty. She wanted him buried deep inside, bruising her with his strength.

"Take me," she moaned.

Reaching around, he unfastened her shirt. He trailed kisses along her shoulder, removing her shirt with his mouth as his hands freed her breasts. "Do you want to play?"

"Yessss," she hissed, too needy to fight.

He smiled. "Not so fast, we have plenty of time," he said. Nuzzling against her neck, his fingers found her nipples. Gently pulling and tugging, he coaxed them to attention.

Teasing, tormenting, tantalizing and totally arousing. Shelley's knees weakened. She leaned into Talcor's strength and moaned, "Touch me, please, please, please."

"Agree to accept my collar and I will," he whispered into her ear, following the words with his tongue. She instinctively tried to pull away from the sensations flooding her but he held her tightly as he continued lashing her ear with his warm, wet tongue.

Lost in his touch, it took a moment for Shelley to process his words. When she did, it was as if a cold shower flooded her heated body.

"What did you say?" she gasped out, not believing that any modern man could be so barbaric, even a Darinthian.

He chuckled. "You heard me."

"No way will you ever collar me! That's barbaric."

"Do you really think you can defy me? You almost said 'yes' and I've barely touched you."

Shelley gulped. He was right. How was she going to fight him? A traitorous part of her mind whispered that she really didn't want to fight. This man was her fantasy come to life. Didn't she want to know exactly what he could do to her? Didn't she want to experience sex like the women in the vids?

She closed her eyes and shuddered. What was she thinking? This man was dangerous. He knew where Marissa was and what was happening to her. This man was not a sex toy to be used and discarded. He'd never accept that role. He'd always demand control and Shelley simply wasn't ready to cede control to any man, at least not willingly. She had no doubt that he could convince her of anything but she'd make him work for it. She wouldn't just give in.

Shelley felt Talcor's muscles bulge as he tightened his arm around her waist. His musky, masculine scent rolled over her, smothering her with desire. Her stomach roiled. What would he do next? And why was she just letting this happen? She wasn't a bimbo like those in the vids. She wasn't so easily seduced.

"How long has it been?" he whispered.

"How long for what?"

"How long since a man has satisfied you?"

"Define satisfied." Shelley felt his chest rumble with laughter.

"If you have to ask, then I can assume you've never been satisfied. What is wrong with the men on your world that your desires and needs go unmet?" he murmured softly. Wrapping a fist in her hair, he gently pulled her head back until their eyes met. "That's a shame. Would you like to change that situation?"

Startled, her eyes widened. Would she? You bet she would. Could she? That was the real question. Could she have sex with this hard stranger? Sex yes, she decided, but this claiming nonsense was too much.

The bulge of his cock pressed against her back. She wanted that cock.

Shelley clenched her thighs in a desperate attempt to quell the heat building between her legs. Then, realizing she was on the brink of being lost, Shelley stiffened and twisted, freeing herself from Talcor's grip, knowing he'd let her go. She never could have broken away without his cooperation. He was too strong. She moved away from him so she could think again.

Shelley backed farther into the room, desperately trying to get some distance between them. With bravado she really didn't feel, she attacked. "I'm not one of your Darinthian women, content to be your plaything. Let me talk to Marissa and then let me go!"

Talcor's grin faded and his eyes narrowed. "It is far too late for you to ever leave."

"What do you mean?"

"You felt the binding. It is not something treated lightly on Darinth."

"I'm not responsible for your barbaric beliefs and I won't be held by them."

"Oh, I think you'll have no choice. Even now, as you sputter against your situation, your pussy is dripping and you want nothing more than to feel what my toys can do to you."

He laughed before turning and locking the door, the snick of the lock loud in the silent torture chamber. She was now a captive but her fear was tinged with lust. She couldn't stop watching him. Poetry, that's what he was, just pure poetry. Graceful and controlled, like some kind of large cat and Shelley just knew that grace carried into the bedroom. Even if she hadn't seen the vid of him controlling Pella's responses, she'd have known this man knew how to pleasure a woman.

His eyes glinted as they met hers.

Shelley's face flushed and she turned to inspect his toys, to escape his knowing eyes.

"To answer your earlier question, satisfied means a mind-blowing orgasm where you scream and writhe, unable to do anything but respond to a man and scream his name as you come. Where you beg him to do it again because once is not enough. Where the pleasure is so intense that it borders on pain and the pain becomes pleasurable. Have you ever known that kind of satisfaction?"

Shelley tried to clear the lump from her throat. She'd never had sex as he described. Sex was typically a tame thing where her mind never shut off and she considered herself lucky if she even got wet before the man shoved his cock into her pussy.

"I don't believe you've ever been satisfied," he said.

Furious at the accuracy of his statement, Shelley picked up the dildo that lay on the counter and threw it at him. Before she could find another object to send flying, Talcor was on her.

His tackle swung her around and carried her to the floor. Grabbing her wrists, he yanked them over her head. Holding them with one hand, his other captured her chin, forcing her eyes to meet his. "I see I will have to teach you the benefits of believing in Darinthian customs."

Chapter Eight

ᐂ

Shelley struggled to move but Talcor's pelvis kept her pressed to the floor. His weight was an unyielding pressure, too heavy for her to escape. Rage bubbled up and she exploded. "Is this what happened to Marissa? Was she held captive and raped? Is that why you don't want me to talk to her? Because I'd discover your crime?"

"Before I'm through with you, you will admit the power of the binding." Standing, he yanked her to her feet and dragged her to the table.

"No! Let me go!" She tried to evade but Talcor was too strong and too fast. Ignoring her screams and demands, he forced her to the table. He held her down until the fastenings could take over.

The leather bands around her wrists and ankles had no give. A small tendril of fear curled in Shelley's belly as she realized just how helpless and vulnerable she'd become. Sure, Jared was somewhere in the house but she knew he couldn't do anything to stop Talcor. And it was becoming painfully obvious to Shelley that she couldn't expect help from anyone else on this planet.

"Let me go," she demanded again. "This is rape!" Waiting for a reply, she realized how empty the room felt. He hadn't just left her here, had he? "Let me go," she shouted as loudly as she was able, trying to stretch her neck to spot Talcor's location. She couldn't quite see and she felt nothing. She drew in a breath to shout again only to have a hand placed over her mouth. A voice whispered in her ear.

"I can assure you that by the time I finally take you, it won't be rape," Talcor said. He stepped back and smiled down at Shelley, a smile that did nothing to lessen her fear. Reaching behind him, he picked up a knife.

"N-no..." stuttered Shelley, barely able to speak over her fear. Talcor's face had hardened. No trace of warmth remained. He moved toward her, the knife held in front of him. He met her eyes as he lowered it.

Shelley was terrified of knives. She'd been cut once, and expecting to feel the bite of the knife, nearly fainted when Talcor started cutting away her clothes.

"I want see all of you."

Shelley bit her lip. Being naked was fine if it meant he'd put the knife down soon. She closed her eyes, trying to regain her balance.

She could feel Talcor methodically removing all her clothes, including her shoes. She couldn't prevent herself from squirming when he trailed a finger up her slit or when he pinched one of her nipples. The fear accompanying her arousal was unlike anything she'd ever experienced. Sure, she'd wanted to play games with Talcor but this wasn't a game. They both knew that despite her protests, he could do anything he wanted. It added a level of sexual tension that Shelley had fantasized about but never believed possible.

How could she still want this man when he created such paralyzing fear? The mixture of arousal and panic took her breath away, making it hard to think and even harder to put up any kind of fight.

Not helping her struggle were Talcor's murmurings. "Have you ever felt pain and pleasure at the same time? Has any man ever forced his will on you? Have you always been in control? Have you ever had anal sex? Have you ever used nipple clamps? Dildos? Have you ever been whipped?"

Obviously Talcor didn't expect answers since he didn't once pause for her reply. It was almost as if he were inventorying the things he planned to do to her. Even the thought of some of them sent need arcing along her spine. She longed to yell at him to shut up but she finally realized that it might be time for a little caution.

Lightly massaging her breasts, he said, "I'm glad your breasts are not augmented. Augmented breasts tend to lose sensation and I want you to feel everything I'm going to do to you."

Then he stepped back and tilted his head as if planning his next move. Eyes burning, he slowly walked around her, examining every inch of her body. Shelley could feel the trail of his gaze. She felt her face flame and wasn't sure if it was caused by lust or embarrassment. Her nipples tightened. She realized no man had ever really looked at her before, not like this. Talcor, taking his time, inspected every detail of her body and just when she thought she'd scream with tension, he said, "You're beautiful."

The empty aching in her pelvis was nearly unbearable.

Talcor took another step back from the table and placed the knife on a counter. He longed to force her surrender, to make her beg for completion. He could do it. He had the power. He also knew it would be a mistake. As much as he longed to fulfill his needs, as much as Shelley wanted the same, she wasn't quite ready to go so far.

Talcor's mind raced as he struggled to control his lust. He couldn't just force Shelley's cooperation. He'd never raped a woman but then he'd never been in the grip of such a strong binding before. All his previous women, including Pella, had liked the pain and pleasure mixture that was his trademark. Many women had accepted the first stage of the binding for a chance to be with him. He wasn't used to a woman's refusal. Shelley's struggles could easily push him over the edge to pure violence and he hesitated, not quite sure how to resist the allure that brute force offered. The more Shelley struggled, the more he wanted to take her with no finesse, no gentleness. He had to gain her cooperation and pure lust alone wouldn't solve the problem.

Shelley didn't realize that the binding only occurred if two people were compatible. Yes, the first step of the binding could be performed with anyone but the driving need he felt to collar her only happened when the ritual could go all the way to the third step. How did he explain that to an off-worlder who, judging by her expression, simply wanted to kill him after she fucked him?

If he took her with violence, without first capturing her mind, it would make a mockery of the binding and that he could not, would not do. He would never betray his customs. After seeing Kytar and Marissa, he knew Shelley's background made it impossible to treat her as a Darinthian woman. She simply didn't have the upbringing to understand the binding. He knew she'd fight it and him, even if she wanted what he offered. As his mind processed possibilities, his raging need calmed a little, enough to plot his next move. Shelley must learn that he was in charge.

Talcor looked at her, spread on the table like a pagan offering. How many other woman had he seen in the same position? Many, many women had experienced his particular predilections but none of them had moved him the way Shelley did. The glistening curls between her legs an intense echo of the hair falling nearly to the floor. She glared at him with a mixture of fear and arousal. Talcor was sure she'd never felt the combination before. *Mine, all mine, even if she won't yet admit it,* he thought with satisfaction. Knowing he had to be careful, that his needs were raging almost out of control, he thought about how to convince Shelley to say yes to his collar.

"Shelley," he whispered, "perhaps a trade will ease your mind."

Startled by his soft voice, Shelley ceased struggling against her bindings. "A trade?"

"Give me ten minutes. If you still say no after ten minutes, I'll release you and not touch you again."

Shelley's heart raced. Was he serious? Only ten minutes? She could easily resist him for that long, couldn't she? No man had aroused her to mindless pleasure in such a short period of time, and as long as she could think, she'd tell him no. Her impulsive nature nearly had her saying yes then she hesitated. Everything on Darinth was different. What was the catch? The trick she was sure he'd spring on her the minute she said yes? "And if after ten minutes I say yes?"

"Then I'll give you pleasure like you've never known before."

"That's all?" A shaky laugh escaped. "And if I say no, you stop? You stop forever and let me leave Darinth? No other tricks?"

"No tricks but you should know that Darinthian magic means that at some point during the ten minutes you'll agree to accept my collar and we'll be free to move through the second stage of the binding."

"That's not going to happen. If I accept this deal, I want you to promise that the vid recording device is off. I've no desire to star in one of your little productions."

"That's not under my control."

"What do you mean?"

"The magic on our planet works in its own ways. There may or may not be a record of our ritual binding. The vids just appear, usually in an elder's office. Besides, what does it matter? On Darinth such things are normal and accepted, indeed a source of pride in our customs."

"Then I won't accept because it is not a custom on our world!"

"Shelley, I offer you a way to escape. There is no other way. If you do not agree to my proposal, then I'll just seduce you until you agree to everything I ask and I will take as long as necessary to do so. Your choice. Accept the bargain or be prepared to surrender your will to mine, even if it takes days. Surely, you're not afraid of being unable to last ten minutes with me?"

Shelley laughed, refusing to show her doubt and confusion. She could stay focused. She would stay focused. She pretended she was confident in her ability to say "no" when saying "yes" meant being tied to this barbarian forever with no hope of escaping the accursed planet. "Then I guess I have no choice but to accept your proposal."

Her heart stuttered when she saw the look of triumph on Talcor's face. "Your acceptance is noted."

"What do you mean by that statement?"

"The magic — the magic you don't believe in — will hold us to our bargain no matter what happens in our ten minutes."

Barely daring to breathe, Shelley watched Talcor. His eyes had narrowed to blue ice chips and Shelley fought the realization that she might have made yet another mistake. She was truly helpless.

No one was going to rescue her from this impulsive belief that she could resist Talcor. She watched as a thin smile crept across his face and he turned to open a drawer. She could hear him rummaging through it, obviously looking for something, grunting with satisfaction when he found it. Then he turned and walked back toward her.

"Your eyes are too bold," he stated. "Darinthian women cast coy, sexual or flirtatious looks, not defiant challenges because Darinthian men are conditioned to dominate any woman who issues such a challenge. For your own safety, I'm covering your eyes." Calmly reaching forward, he placed a mask over her eyes.

"No!" Shelley's heart stuttered as he blindfolded her.

"Oh yes," hissed Talcor. "I'll not make the same mistake as Kytar. You will accept my authority and you'll do it quickly."

What did he mean by that statement? In her current state, she couldn't make sense of it so she dismissed it. With a sinking feeling, she realized she was captive in a dungeon filled with dangerous toys and a very dangerous man. Even more horrifying was her immediate response to her situation. Her pussy flooded with juices and tightened into a nearly unbearable need. "Take the blindfold off!"

"I like to hear my women moan with desire and shout with the pain and pleasure I give them so I rarely use a gag. However, I do not want to hear senseless demands. If you continue, I'll gag you. Your choice. Nod if you understand me."

Shelley hesitated then nodded and bit her tongue to still the protests bubbling to the surface. The blindfold was bad enough. She certainly didn't want a gag too. She needed to stay focused and ignore things she couldn't change.

Even as Shelley tried to regain her breath and calm her racing heart, he lifted her chin and fastened a wide band around her throat. Then she felt a band around her waist. She tried to squirm but the bindings made movement nearly impossible. She was well and truly helpless, blind to know what was coming.

Shelley felt the table move under her hips. Oh no! Talcor was spreading the slats. Her legs moved outward. She felt the strain in her hips. Cold air hit her labia. With her arms spread wide, cunt wide open and no give in any of the straps, Shelley felt vulnerable and exposed, as well as aroused, she reluctantly admitted. Her pelvis clenched with need and he hadn't even really touched her yet. *Focus! Focus*, she ordered herself.

She still had her mind. He might have captured her body but he hadn't taken her mind. *Not yet*, whispered a traitorous voice in her head. She briefly debated just bowing to his will and domination, making it easy on herself, but Shelley had never taken the easy way out of anything.

"Our ten minutes starts now," purred Talcor, obviously pleased with Shelley's situation.

Shelley stilled at his words, preparing to do battle, wondering how much pain he'd cause. She was totally unprepared for the soft touch of Talcor's lips against her nipple. Barely a breath of a touch, her pelvis arched of the table. Before she had a chance to relax, he did the same with the other nipple. She felt her breasts flood with longing, aching for a harder touch that didn't come. Instead, Talcor's mouth breathed along her abdomen, trailing to her belly button. A quick push of his tongue, gone before she'd even had a chance to respond, working its way ever lower.

Gentle hands stroked her thighs, avoiding her dripping cunt and aching core. Shelley arched her pelvis, hoping for a quick lick or a firm piercing. Instead she felt cold metal parting her labia. She tried to jerk back but the band at her waist held her firm as Talcor's lips trailed back up her abdomen.

Shelley struggled to make sense of the sensations assaulting her opening. The cold metal warmed and seemed to liquefy at the same time, holding her open to the room and anything Talcor might want to do with her. Even as his lips worked their way back up her body, feathery-light touches massaged her cunt. What was that thing he had put in her? She'd never felt anything like it—intoxicating, not enough to help her come but it never ever let her forget her exposure.

"What is that?" she whispered, unable to maintain any kind of indifference in the face of the assault.

Talcor chuckled. "Just something I invented to remind my woman that she is open to me and under my control. Right now it is set to give pleasure and I can see you like it. Don't get too comfortable though. I prefer some of the other settings."

Shelley tensed as the device started emitting a low thrum. She realized it was a vibrator but one quite unlike her toys at home. This vibrator echoed deep within. She felt a small pulsation that increased in intensity until her bones vibrated in time with the machine. It felt good but Shelley quickly realized the vibrations weren't enough to help her climax. The vibrations sent her up toward an orgasm, an orgasm that was tantalizingly out of reach. She tried to squirm, to increase the pressure.

Meanwhile, Talcor's hands wrapped around her breasts, gently massaging, causing her mind to split between the sensations below and above her waist. Warmth flooded every vein, forcing a moan rather than a verbal reply.

Shelley's cunt tightened with need as the relentless vibration continued. Her abdomen clenched as Talcor's hands moved to massage her belly, forcing a protest when her breasts were abandoned. She longed to rip off the blindfold so she could see what he was doing. Her cunt clenched in a spasm that was nearly painful.

Still spread wide, she felt so empty. She needed to be filled. As if sensing her need, the device at her cunt suddenly sent a probe into her vagina. In and out so fast, but it was too thin to give her the satisfaction she craved. Another light, breathy taunting of her nipples set her screaming, "Touch them harder! Please, this is torture!"

"My invention not only gives pleasure," he said.

Shelley struggled to make sense of his words when she felt an intense pain, as though she'd been plugged into an electric socket. She gasped in a breath while Talcor licked her nipples. The combination of pain and pleasure unlike anything she'd ever felt before. The device rapidly flickered between vibration and shock before settling back to vibration only. Shelley moaned, her cunt clenched, forehead dripping with sweat, she ached for an orgasm to release the awful tension in her body.

Talcor's hands moved to surround her breasts.

"Beg," whispered Talcor.

"What..."

"You want me to touch your nipples, don't you?"

Shelley remained silent.

"Beg me to touch you," he said as his fingertips circled her nipples.

Shelley swallowed, trying to get rid of the hard lump in her throat. "Please..." she started, but couldn't finish.

Another round of shock and vibration rippled through her abdomen.

"Please what?" Talcor prompted, whispering in her ear and then reaching out to nibble on it.

"Please touch me," Shelley managed to stammer.

"Where?" Talcor continued his assault on her ear.

Shelley struggled to think past the shivery sensations threatening to overwhelm her. "My nipples," she gasped, "please touch my nipples."

"See, that wasn't so hard, was it?" Talcor said as he caught a nipple between his fingers and leaned over to lick it.

Shelley arched, unable to cope with the stunning stab of desire in her pelvis.

"Harder! Touch me harder! Please…"

"Not yet," he said, and he lowered his head back to her nipples. He nipped and sucked then sucked hard, grazing her nipples with his teeth before biting then licking. His relentless attention soon had her nipples hurting. They simply weren't used to such incessant stimulation.

At the same time, the device continued its relentless vibration. Her mind struggled to make sense of the pain and pleasure combination. Her nipples hurt. Her cunt ached with pleasure. She'd just about accepted the combination when Talcor changed it. The device in her cunt sent a series of painful shocks at the same time that Talcor softened his attack on her nipples. Shelley screamed. Her body afire and inflamed with need. Still Talcor didn't stop. He ignored her moans, her demands and her pleas as he sent alternating sensations coursing through her body.

Shelley was sure she'd go insane when something inside snapped and she felt the pain change. The device holding her cunt open expanded, spreading her farther, emphasizing her emptiness. She caught her breath as the pain morphed into a pleasurable intensity, blanking all thought at the same time that Talcor removed her blindfold.

"Shelley, look at me," she heard as if from a great distance. She blinked her eyes and struggled to understand the voice.

"Shelley," the voice whispered. "Shelley, come back to me."

Shelley shuddered as she realized Talcor was calling to her. He smiled down at her.

Her body ached with unsatisfied need. She closed her eyes and drew in a deep breath then opened her eyes and met his smile.

"You're driving me crazy," she said, still trying to stay in control.

"Yes, isn't it wonderful?" he countered.

Shelley stared at him, wondering how to reply, wondering if he'd ever satisfy her. "I can't take much more," she warned.

"Oh I think you'll be very surprised by just how much you can take," he whispered. Lowering his head, he gently kissed her. "We're just starting."

Shelley felt a sliver of unease, but before she could process it, Talcor turned his attention back to her nipples. Again and again he brought her close to a climax, always denying her the final release. Every time she faded into the sensations he effortlessly created, as pain and pleasure merged, he called her back. Until finally, tears escaped her eyes and she mindlessly begged him to satisfy her, to ease the ache he'd created. Still he ignored her and continued his ministrations.

Every muscle in Shelley's body clenched and released as she tried desperately to find some satisfaction.

"Are you ready?" Talcor whispered.

Shelley felt him move a little and his hand cupped her mound. She nearly sobbed with relief as she felt the pressure of his hand. She tried to move into it, to stimulate herself. He laughed and moved his hand. "Yes, I guess you are ready."

"Please, please..." Shelley moaned, tossing her head back and forth. Her pussy burned with need even as her juices flowed freely and accumulated under her butt. Her nipples ached. She tried to squirm, trying to get some—any—satisfaction but it eluded her even as her need built more. She'd never felt such a raging, blinding need. When all the stimulation suddenly stopped she forgot her bargain with Talcor and screamed, "Don't stop!"

"Are you sure," whispered Talcor in her ear. She quickly turned her head, trying to kiss him but he moved out of reach. "Shelley, are you sure you don't want me to stop?"

"I'm sure, damn you! Don't leave me hanging like this."

Talcor, intoxicated by the sight of Shelley writhing with need, took a deep breath and focused on the purpose of their bargain. "Do you accept my collar?" Talcor whispered in her ear as he continued his light touches on her breast.

Wordlessly, Shelley shook her head. She couldn't take that step...could she?

Talcor stroked Shelley's abdomen, leaving a trail of fire in his wake.

"Please, please, please," begged Shelley. "I can't take any more. I need release. Please, Talcor. Please let me come."

"Say the words. Say you accept my collar."

"Yes," screamed Shelley, "yes, damn you! I accept your collar! Please Talcor...please don't stop. I'll accept your collar...anything...only please, please let me come!"

Talcor gently trailed a kiss along Shelley's face. "Such beautiful begging deserves a reward," he said, reaching her ear, running his tongue around its whorls at the same time that his hand removed the device from her vagina. Before she felt the emptiness, three fingers entered her. A quick, sudden sharp pain in her nipples sent her soaring while the fingers in her cunt finished the job and her entire body clenched into one blinding spasm of release. Wave after wave of release followed until her vision faded and she knew nothing except the pleasure flooding her body and the hard body that held her safe.

Chapter Nine

ဢ

Jared rolled out of bed and landed on his knees. Holding his head in his hands, too exhausted to stand, he groaned. What had happened? His memory returned and he snorted. He knew the answer to that question. Pella had happened. Darinthian magic had happened. Whether he chose to believe in it or not, there was no denying the effect of it. Even now he wondered where Pella had disappeared to and when they could climb back into this magnificent bed. What was it about Pella that made him forget everything but her? Even Shelley, he realized.

How could he have forgotten the danger Shelley was in? How could he take his pleasure with Pella? True, they hadn't had actual intercourse but they'd come close and Jared still ached for Pella. He'd never felt such an intense reaction to a woman. How much truth was there to this Darinthian magic stuff? Shelley, he yanked his thoughts away from Pella. Shelley was in danger and he'd promised to help. Instead, here he was lusting after Talcor's woman. How could he do that?

He flopped back up on the bed, feeling guilty, lower than a rat. He rolled over and something crinkled underneath him. He moved aside so he could pick up the paper. His heart raced, Pella had left him a note. He smiled, once again forgetting Shelley.

* * * * *

Shelley woke alone in a strange bedroom. The memory of Talcor's masterful playing of her body rushed back. Her face heated at the memory.

She rolled over and groaned. Her body felt a little stiff, as if she'd been working out too hard. Not surprising, given the intensity of the orgasm that had shaken her to the point of unconsciousness and he hadn't even entered her. Shelley wondered if she'd survive the entry of his cock, given what he'd managed with his hands and talented mouth.

She'd begged him to satisfy her. How could she have done that? With a growing sense of horror, she remembered his other insistent demand. She'd been lost in the haze of arousal. Had she surrendered everything? With a sinking feeling, she knew she'd agreed to accept his collar. How could she do that?

Slowly, she raised her hand to her neck, expecting to find a collar, though she didn't feel one. Her hand touched bare neck. *Why didn't he collar me?* Just as she thought the question, Talcor entered the bedroom.

"I left you a robe and sandals in the bathroom," he said, nodding back the way he'd come. Then he noticed her hand position. A wry grin on his face, Talcor crossed his arms over his broad chest and leaned back against the door. Cocking an eyebrow, he asked, "Wondering where your collar is? Are you ready for it?"

She frowned.

Walking over, he sat beside her.

She quickly lowered her hand, nervous and unsure about what would come next. She wished he hadn't seen her gesture but she refused to surrender so easily. "Never," she replied softly, keeping her eyes on Talcor.

"It is too late to withdraw your acceptance," he said in a soft voice.

Shelley looked at the powerful man sitting next to her. His arms bulged with muscle, his broad chest defined, his legs nearly as large as her waist. She'd never felt a man's strength before, the power to simply take what he wanted, and she thought, with a thrill of desire, that he wanted her but did he love her?

"Are you still going to fight me?"

Shelley realized she didn't want to fight him. She thought she should but she didn't care about that anymore. She'd thrilled to his masterful control of her. She couldn't lie to him and tell him she hadn't enjoyed what he'd done. Besides, he'd seen her response. He knew his power. She shook her head.

Talcor's head tilted, eyebrow lifting, questioning her response.

"I'm not going to fight. What's the point? You've demonstrated that you're stronger than I am."

"And did you enjoy that demonstration?" he asked, his voice still soft.

Shelley frowned. She didn't want to answer him.

"Shelley, did you like what I did?"

She closed her eyes, her chest tight, head spinning as she honestly answered, "Yes. Yes, I enjoyed it very much."

"Why was that admission so hard for you? Sex should be pleasurable."

Shelley opened her eyes and met his blue gaze. He seemed sincerely curious. She shrugged. "On my world, men and women are equal."

"But how can that be? Men and women are different. Each has strengths and weaknesses. Clearly, you are not as strong as I am physically. How can you pretend otherwise..." he trailed off. His eyes narrowed. "Jared is the result, isn't he? You've managed equality by castrating your males."

Shelley gulped in the face of his anger. She'd never thought of it quite like that.

"Make no mistake—you will never be my equal. You are my companion and respected as such. Your strengths will be valued and respected. You will in turn accord my strengths the same value and respect."

Shelley felt a rush of longing as she asked, "It works both ways?"

Talcor tilted his head and narrowed his eyes. "Of course it does. How else could it work?"

"Does...you said...you said I was yours...that means you are also mine?"

Talcor leaned back against the bedpost. "Yes. The magic of the binding ties us. I am every bit as much yours as you are mine."

"And when we're...tied...what happens then? What happens to my job? My family? Will I ever be able to see them again? How can I take someone like you home to meet my parents?"

"We will work everything out. You are my companion. I will take care of your needs — all your needs."

"Then what about my biggest need, the one that drove me to this horrible planet? When will I be able to talk to Marissa?"

Talcor emitted an exclamation of frustration. Suddenly he moved forward, capturing both her wrists and pulling them over her head. Leaning down, he covered her mouth with his, forcing his tongue between her teeth as his chest flattened her breasts, creating a clawing ache Shelley could barely breathe through. Shelley tried to think. She tried to fight. But only for a moment before she relaxed into the sensations that Talcor elicited so easily. Becoming lost in his mouth and the feel of his hands on her wrists and the pressure of his chest, she realized she didn't want to fight this man. She wanted to surrender to his strength, just as she had in her vision. As that thought flittered through her mind, Talcor released her, leaving her frustrated.

Standing, he said, "If you behave, maybe I'll let you talk to Marissa when she's available and if Kytar agrees. Now enough of Marissa. You have other things to think of at the moment. You are mine. Fight all you like, it won't change the outcome." He held her eyes for a long moment before turning, leaving the room and slamming the door.

Talcor stopped in the hallway and looked back at the closed door, fighting down a wave of disappointment. There'd be no collaring today. Shelley had surrendered to his power but she hadn't accepted it. He wanted a companion who admitted their bonds, not one he'd be forever fighting. After he'd demonstrated his control, he'd foolishly thought that Shelley would be more interested in him than in Marissa.

He shook his head. It didn't matter. She'd agreed to accept his collar even if he wouldn't give it to her today. She belonged to him and he would make sure that he filled her thoughts. She'd be too busy in the next few days to worry about Marissa. He could wait. He'd force himself to wait until he had her complete cooperation and acceptance, maybe even her love.

* * * * *

Shelley stared at the closed door, aching with need. How dare he leave her like this? Fuming as her cunt clenched in a violent spasm of need. *Get a grip,* she told herself. She'd never needed a man before, so why should that change now?

Her hand crept to her slit to find it dripping wet, aching from last night's play and from the simple kiss today. How could he elicit such a response when he was such a jerk? Her clit throbbed. She fantasized that it was Talcor's hand on her, rubbing and soothing the ache deep within. She lost herself in pleasure as she reached the first peak then the second. Gradually dosing off after satisfying her immediate needs, she resolved that she wouldn't let Talcor disturb her. He wasn't going to have that power over her.

Shelley startled as the door opened again a few moments later. Eyes closed, she cringed, hoping it wasn't Talcor coming back. She was certain he'd know what she'd been up to and she didn't want to admit he'd left her so needy. Slitting open her eyes, she relaxed. It wasn't Talcor.

Jared entered the room and moved to stand at the side of her bed. His pained expression alarmed her and she felt a twinge of guilt. Talcor had driven all thought of Jared from her head. What had been happening to him? "Jared, what's wrong?"

"You mean other than the fact that we're virtual prisoners here? What could be wrong?"

"I don't know but you don't look very happy."

"I…" he trailed off, and shook his head before changing the subject. "Breakfast will be ready soon."

Shelley wasn't going to be put off by his prevarication. She knew him too well.

"Jared, what's wrong?"

He hesitated then said, "We've never dated others."

"No…so?"

"Maybe it's time we do."

"What?"

"Look, Talcor threatened me. He told me if I touched you at all that he'd make sure you suffered."

"He doesn't have any right to dictate to either one of us," hissed Shelley. Angry and upset by her response to Talcor, she knew she shouldn't berate Jared. It wasn't Jared's fault he wasn't strong enough to fight Talcor. It wasn't Jared's fault that Talcor controlled her.

As if sensing her thoughts, Jared said, "Well, in case you haven't noticed, he's a lot stronger than me and he seems to have the law on his side."

Shelley's jaw clenched. She couldn't deny those facts, as much as she might like to.

"Maybe it would be better if we weren't a couple right now."

"That's it? We're done?"

"That's not it. You know we'll always be friends but we stayed together more out of convenience than love."

"Why does that bother you now? Are you afraid of Talcor?"

"I don't want to see you hurt and I'm convinced he'll follow through on his threat."

Shelley shook her head. "That's no reason to give in to him."

Jared closed his eyes, a grimace flashing across his face before he met her eyes. "We've never lied to each other…"

"What else, Jared? What else is bothering you?"

He took a deep breath before saying, "I'm attracted to Pella."

"You're what?"

"Pella…she's beautiful. Something about her just calls to me. I want to be with her."

A roaring wave of rage engulfed Shelley as she spit out, "She's a mindless little drone. Is physical beauty really enough for you?"

Before Jared could reply, Shelley continued. "Did you ever think that maybe Talcor set you up so you'd do this very thing and if Talcor warned you off me, how do you think he's going to feel about you hitting on Pella?"

Shelley took a deep breath to continue the argument but Jared held up a hand.

"Don't talk about her like that. She's sweet, really sweet. She's never hurt you and I won't listen to you take your anger at Talcor out on her."

"I didn't mean—"

"Yes, you did. I'm sorry, Shelley. Pella is as stunned as I am. I don't believe it was a setup and I don't believe Talcor will get angry. Hell, he told Pella to take care of my needs. I know this is a lousy time to break up but I have to pursue my feelings for Pella," he said, and then turned and walked out.

Shocked by the fact that Jared had stood up to her, Shelley stared at the closed bedroom door. Jared—nice simple Jared—had just broken up with her. Sure, he'd never met her needs, not really, but he'd always been there for her.

Jared was right. It was a hell of a time to break up. She felt threatened by Talcor and the only thing that had stood between them was Jared. Now he was gone, neatly removed from the game, and Shelley couldn't help wondering, despite Jared's denial, if Talcor had deliberately set up this scenario and if Pella really cared about Jared the way Jared seemed to care for her.

Feeling lonely and a little lost, Shelley climbed out of bed.

She walked into the bathroom. Taking a cool shower, she tried to wash away her need for Talcor. Stubbornly, he remained in her head. Reaching for the robe hanging near the shower, she donned it, barely noticing its richness until she'd put it on.

Gleaming like satin, she was startled by the fact that it felt like fur on the inside. Its jade-green sheen complemented her complexion and she wondered if Talcor had left it for that very reason. Unable to find an excuse to remain in the bedroom, Shelley slipped into her sandals and made her way downstairs.

Pella met her at the bottom of the stairs. "You have a visitor," she said, waving toward the library.

"A visitor? Marissa? Is Marissa here?" she asked. Not waiting for an answer, she raced to the library and stopped dead with disappointment as she realized it wasn't Marissa who stood looking out the window.

Shelley recognized the man when he turned away from the window. Davo. Elderly but not old, he looked like a kindly gentleman. Shelley knew that assessment wasn't accurate. Even so, she couldn't prevent the thrill of happiness that ran through her. Despite the fact that he hadn't been helpful and was part of the reason she was trapped on this forsaken planet, she was happy to see someone she knew. Maybe she could stay with him and get away from Talcor.

She nearly ran to his arms until she noticed his face. Davo's eyebrows rose as he looked at her. He smiled and his gaze carried all the male lust that she'd come to associate with Darinthian males. "Do you realize that is a companion robe you wear?"

Shelley stiffened.

"I did warn you not to come."

She decided to ignore his comments. "You'll help me, won't you?" she asked. "I want to speak to Marissa."

"My daughter is a lucky woman to have such a loyal friend," said Davo as he walked to her. Shelley tried to evade him but he easily enveloped her in a big hug. Then he kissed her on both cheeks, took both her hands and stepped back a little.

She felt uncomfortable with his familiarity. Shoving aside her unease, she knew she just needed to stay focused on her purpose and she'd be okay. "I want to speak to Marissa—"

Davo held up a hand and interrupted. "You know that's not going to happen anytime soon. Be happy you're safe."

Shelley felt his warm concern even if she raged at the reason for it. She had just started to relax, thinking him not bad for a Darinthian, when he continued. "You are incredibly lovely. Talcor is a lucky man."

Shelley snapped, "Talcor is a bastard! And this is all your fault. Marissa wouldn't be in a mess and I wouldn't be here if you hadn't told her she was safe!" Shelley shouted, recognizing that Davo's gentle appearance was just on the surface and he was no different than any other Darinthian male.

Davo closed his eyes and took a deep breath. When he opened his eyes, he smiled. "You'd think after Marissa and her mother I'd be used to blunt females but somehow such candor still surprises me. You should have listened to us and simply waited. You've gained nothing by coming to Darinth except your own bonding."

"I'll not be held hostage by your customs."

Davo laughed. "My dear, you are already bound, whether you accept it or not."

Shelley glared at the elderly statesman. She wanted to scream in frustration. Who did these men think they were to treat her like this?

"My dear—"

"I'm not your dear anything!" Shelley exclaimed. "I want to talk to Marissa."

"As soon as she's available, if Talcor and Kytar agree."

"Marissa can make up her own mind. She doesn't need these men to give her permission. Tell her I'm here."

Davo sighed. "You know that is not possible."

"No, I don't know that."

"Certainly Talcor has told you. I know you spoke to the ambassador and he told you too. I am sorry you don't like our customs but you will respect them if only because you have no choice. Talcor has bound you. You may not wear his collar yet but his mark is there. You are anything he wants, whether you are ready to admit that or not. If need be, you'll learn the same way Marissa did."

"What do you mean—the way Marissa did?"

Davo shrugged. "That's for Talcor to teach you."

So much for rescue from this direction, she thought. "I am not a slave. No man controls me!" Shelley screamed at Davo, unable to maintain a façade of calm when every fiber of her being was in rebellion.

"Calm down!"

"No! No! I won't calm down. I want to talk to Marissa and then I want off this planet!"

The library door slammed open as Talcor entered the room and roared, "Enough! Shelley, you're becoming hysterical."

"I'm never hysterical. I'm angry," she retorted.

"I feel you. I feel your every emotion. I felt your masturbation earlier. You are not rational and Davo's visit seems to have upset you further. Go to the dining room, eat breakfast and calm down."

Shelley started at the cold tone in Talcor's voice. Obviously, he wasn't happy with either of them. That he should be unhappy with her was a given, but clearly, something Davo had had said bothered him. What? What secret had he revealed that Shelley had missed?

"I'm not a child, to be sent out of the room—"

"Act like a spoiled child and I'll treat you like one," Talcor said. He grabbed her face between his hands, stared deeply into her eyes, and said, "Go eat breakfast and calm down."

Shelley wanted to scream at him but didn't quite dare. Her anger leaked away.

Shaking his head, he said, "This conversation is over, Shelley. Go."

She stared at him, unmoving.

"Now," he said in a soft voice that brooked no disagreement.

He removed his hands and nodded toward the door. Unnerved by his apparent control and the thought that he might actually be able to feel her emotions, Shelley threw a glare at Davo before fleeing the room.

Chapter Ten

❧

Talcor and Davo watched Shelley leave then Davo turned to Talcor. "She's even more independent than Marissa."

"And I'm stronger than Kytar. I won't let her challenge me. I don't want her to know anything about Marissa's defiance. You nearly let it slip."

Marissa had challenged Kytar for her freedom. If a woman wanted to renounce her link to her mate and he refused to release her, she could formally ask for the challenge ritual. The challenge ritual tested the link between bonded pairs. The Darinthian male was allowed to fight the challenge—fight to keep his woman under his control. Though not allowed to have intercourse with her for the duration of the challenge, he would have two weeks to train her. To do anything else he wanted. Anything.

Darinthian males typically controlled themselves, but during challenge training there were no such safeguards for the women. If a woman demanded the ritual, it meant that the dominant male could do anything he wanted to consolidate the binding—in a very public venue.

Davo raised his eyebrows and shrugged. Talcor's mouth curved in what looked like a reluctant grin. Davo laughed. "Talcor, it's obvious she's already challenging you."

Running a hand through his thick hair, Talcor grinned ruefully. "True, but there's a world of difference between a formal challenge and this defiance. Besides, I've barely started."

"Yes, why haven't you gone further? I can feel she's accepted your collar. Finish the binding."

"Pella and I have unfinished business. Besides, Shelley's not quite ready. I've chosen to wait a few days."

"I don't think that's necessary."

"What do you mean?"

"Your bond with her is even stronger than Kytar's and Marissa's, as I'm sure you've felt. Why not finish it?"

"This binding took me by surprise. I expected the first stage link. I didn't expect to be permanently bound with an off-worlder. I don't quite know how to handle her. I'm not Kytar. I'm not you. I don't share your fondness for off-worlders. Part of me wants to deny the connection. How can I be bound to a woman who has no respect for our customs?"

"You deny the connection? Ignoring it will not make it go away," snorted Davo. "It is up to you to teach her respect."

"I'm making progress. I've already gained her acceptance of the collar."

"Then don't follow Kytar's example. Don't give her the chance to defy you. Finish this!"

"You've seen the way she is," Talcor spit out, clearly frustrated by Shelley's continued resistance. "I'll bind her when the time is right."

"You had no qualms about telling Kytar how to handle Marissa. Maybe you should take your own advice. Shelley uses anger to cover her emotions. However, even I felt your connection. Such a strong connection is rare. You should cherish it," Davo said.

"I do cherish it. I cherish it enough not to rush it."

"My apologies, Talcor. I merely came to try to reassure Shelley that Marissa is fine. I meant no disrespect to your house." He bowed his head. "I stand to serve if you have need of me. Good hunting," he said as he turned and left.

Talcor thought about what he'd have to do to tame Shelley. He'd never forced a woman beyond her own limits. He feared Shelley's independence. He didn't know how to bend her will without breaking her. But if he were honest with himself, he knew the magic would not let him ever release her and it took every bit of his self-restraint not to arouse her to the point where she'd agree to anything, just to gain some measure of sexual satisfaction.

He could feel when she masturbated, as she had earlier, and he knew that their encounters aroused her. If he could only push past her belief that she should fight the binding, their union would be an incredible expression of love. But if he pushed her too fast, she wouldn't survive. *Despite Davo's advice and my own to Kytar*, he thought ironically, *the timing isn't quite right. Not yet. Soon but not yet.*

* * * * *

Shelley hesitated halfway to her bedroom. She knew that any safety she felt there was just an illusion. She wasn't safe anywhere on this planet. As she stood, a tantalizing scent created an answering rumble in her stomach. When was the last time she'd eaten? No wonder her body was hungry even if she really didn't feel like eating.

Shelley sighed, resigning herself to following Talcor's orders to get some food when she'd rather defy him. Sighing again, she descended the stairs and followed the scent of food. She entered a room to find a buffet in the far corner. It nearly groaned with voluminous quantities of food. Shelley didn't recognize any of it but the mingled scents were delicious and her stomach grumbled again.

Shelley picked up something orange that looked vaguely like a banana but smelled like a strawberry. Cautiously she licked it. The orange-banana-strawberry thing tasted sweet, unlike anything Shelley had eaten before. She took a bigger bite then quickly finished off the strange fruit.

Shelley started as Pella entered the room from another doorway, carrying yet another dish. She smiled at Shelley. "Please help yourself," she said to Shelley as she placed the dish.

Shelley felt distinctly uncomfortable. She'd seen this woman naked and begging. She'd seen Talcor control this woman. She'd heard Pella's deference to Talcor and it sickened her. Jared had dumped her for this woman. Pella wasn't a person Shelley wanted to be anywhere near.

Pella smiled, and said, "Please eat. The food is safe."

Twit, that's not the reason I hesitated to eat, thought Shelley, determined not to like the woman. Shelley turned back to the food. Reluctant to ask for help but knowing it was stupid not to ask.

"I don't recognize most of this food," Shelley finally said as she stared at a bewildering assortment, stomach growling as the tantalizing scents grew stronger, as if her earlier bite had just woken up her stomach.

Blue food, what kind of food was blue other than blueberries? But the blue food was square, not round. What kind of food was square? The green, yellow, orange and red were at least familiar colors and shapes.

Pella chuckled. "The blue is mirass, a type of fruit. And yes, it grows square. It isn't manufactured that way. The green and yellow ones are vegetables. Orange is a type of egg and red a type of meat. All are compatible with your digestive system."

Shelley stared at the food, its strangeness reminding her of her isolation. Reluctantly, she took a plate and added a few items then sat at the table. After a few bites took the edge off her hunger and stilled her growling stomach, she asked, "Where's Jared?"

Pella blushed as she said, "Jared is on his way."

Shelley ate a few more bites, marveling at the refreshing tang of the blue fruit. Feeling a little better with something in her stomach, she shoved aside her dislike of Pella. Maybe Pella would help her. Jared had said Pella was nice. Now was the perfect opportunity to find out just how nice.

"Pella," Shelley said, "you know I don't belong here, that I'm only looking for my friend. Will you help me escape and find her?"

Pella's smile faded. "Don't be foolish. You don't want to wander around Darinth alone. It's a dangerous place for unprotected females."

"You mean for any female!"

Summer-blue eyes stared at Shelley, steady and unblinking. "No, I said what I meant. Darinth is dangerous for unprotected females and while Talcor may have offered you his protection, if you go out in defiance of him, you won't be safe."

"Pella, please, you have to help me. All I want to do is make sure that Marissa is okay and then I can leave."

Pella shook her head. "Are you not listening to me? Talcor is your protector. You should feel honored. If he feels you need to see your friend, he'll take care of it."

"No, that's not acceptable!"

Pella frowned. "Why will you not accept the fact that Marissa neither needs nor wants your interference? Everyone who saw the challenge ritual knows how Kytar commanded her submission."

Shelley stood and moved toward Pella, leaving her plate of food forgotten on the table. "What are you talking about?"

Pella hesitated. "Didn't Talcor tell you?"

"Tell me what? What is this ritual? The ambassador mentioned it, Talcor didn't."

Pella shook her head. "If Talcor didn't say anything, then it is not my place."

"My friend has been kidnapped. I need to find her. Help me!"

Pella frowned but before she could reply, a masculine voice boomed, "What is going on here?"

Pella squeaked, startled by Talcor's sudden question.

Shelley turned to see Talcor in the doorway. His eyes narrowed into blue lasers.

"Pella, what did you tell her?" he demanded as he moved toward them.

"Don't yell at her," Shelley said, moving in front of Pella as if to protect her.

Pella moved to the side. "I don't need the protection of an off-worlder who knows nothing of our customs!"

Talcor reached Pella and grabbed her arm. "What did you tell her? Did you tell her everything?" He asked softly, even as his muscles clenched in anger.

Pella cringed, but said defiantly, "No Master! She asked but I didn't tell. It is your place to explain our customs."

Talcor's fingers tightened as he glared down at Pella.

"You're hurting me. You're hurting me in anger," Pella said, her voice barely above a whisper.

"Stop tormenting her," Shelley demanded. "She didn't tell me anything and just what was she supposed to hide from me?"

Talcor raised his head, locking his gaze on Shelley before looking back at Pella and loosening his grip. "My apologies, Pella. And, Pella…"

"Yes?"

"We'll talk about last night later."

Pella paled.

Stepping back from Pella, he said, "Go. Now. Make certain Jared does not interrupt. You should enjoy that task and I'm sure you'll find a creative way to entertain him."

Pella closed her eyes.

"Don't worry, just go now," he said, lightly swatting her bottom.

Pella darted around Talcor and headed for the door as Shelley and Talcor glared at each other.

Talcor took a step toward Shelley.

For the first time since reaching Darinth, Shelley hesitated. Had she pushed him too far? She bitterly regretted not listening to everyone's advice. Why had she ever come to this planet? Marissa wouldn't have expected her to place herself in danger. And she certainly felt threatened. Every line of Talcor's body was tense with anger and Shelley eyed him warily as he walked toward her. His muscles bulged and she already knew she was no match for him physically. What was he going to do?

"It is time you learned your place. I had hoped to give you a little more time to adjust but clearly you have no respect for our customs. You denigrate them at every turn. You tried to enlist Davo's help. You try forcing Pella to do things she knows are wrong. This cannot be allowed to continue."

Talcor advanced and Shelley stepped around the table, putting it between them. She didn't know where she was going or how she'd escape but she wouldn't just let Talcor frighten her without a fight.

"Stop," he commanded.

"No," she moaned as she fought, trying to move away from him, but she was unable to break free of his command. Heart thumping, she realized she couldn't fight him.

Talcor reached to the back of her neck, holding her in place while his other hand caressed her collarbone, moving aside her robe. "Do you know why companions wear these robes?"

Shelley startled, even after Davo's earlier comment she hadn't realized the robe was any kind of uniform.

Talcor continued. "Companions wear these robes so their protectors can do this." With a violent downward motion, he ripped the robe off her.

His calm, focused intensity layered with anger frightened her more than she'd thought possible. The trembling started in her knees and worked its way upward as he disposed of her sandals. Standing naked in front of him, unable to stop shivering, she'd never felt so vulnerable. He caught her around the waist as her knees collapsed.

"No," Shelley moaned, still trying to maintain her independence even as she longed to surrender to Talcor's strength. "You have no right to torture me like this. Is this what happened to Marissa? Forced against her will? Kidnapped by one of you barbarians?"

"Enough! It is long past time you forget about Marissa and focus on me." He tightened his grip on Shelley's hair and, pulling down, he forced her to her knees. "Suck my cock," he ordered.

Shelley's lips parted. She whispered, "No," and tried to shake her head but Talcor held her immobile.

"No more games. Suck my cock."

Tears misted her eyes. "Please, not like this…"

"Exactly like this. You tire me by making me repeat myself. For the third time—suck my cock!"

Shelley, frightened by Talcor's intensity, bowed her head and moved her hands to his pants. Her trembling fingers didn't move quite right and Shelley had trouble freeing his cock. Talcor remained stone cold and unmoving, patiently waiting for her to accede to his demand.

He heard her little gasp when she finally saw him fully erect and realized his size. Talcor knew she'd have problems taking all of his cock but at this point he didn't care. And he didn't care about the frisson of fear he could feel running through her. He knew he wouldn't hurt her but it would do her good to wonder and to know that he could only be pushed so far before he'd retaliate. He was stronger and bigger, he was smarter and more determined. She needed to realize he would always win if she chose to make their relationship contentious. She couldn't win this battle, any battle or their war. Ever.

Shelley took Talcor's cock in her hand, wondering how she'd ever fit it into her mouth. She hesitated a second before reaching out with her tongue. Oral sex had never been one of her favorite sex games. Most cocks tasted sour and not at all appetizing, so she wasn't prepared for the taste of Talcor's cock—rich and full, nearly earthy, wholesome and healthy. Shelley quickly lost herself in the different taste of him. Still holding the base of his cock, feeling it pulse in her hand, Shelley moved to the tip and started mouthing it, slowly putting her teeth around it.

"No biting," Talcor said, placing both hands on the sides of her face.

Shelley tried to pull back as Talcor's pelvis moved forward, forcing her mouth wide. Shelley's jaw was on the brink of dislocating when Talcor's hands tightened, two fingers massaging her face, just in front of her ears. Suddenly, a wave of release flooded her and she opened enough to take in a few inches. She closed her eyes, swaying with the sensations flooding her pelvis. It felt like a direct connection between his cock and her cunt, as if each slow stroke filled not only her mouth but her nether region as well. Talcor moved forward, touching the back of her throat, widening it until he could move another inch inside.

Her cunt clenched as he slowly moved forward, filling her until she thought she'd pass out from the pleasure of his determination. She moaned when he pulled back just enough to let her breathe before pushing in again, even deeper.

Again he pulled back. Again he moved forward. Her throat felt bruised, her cunt ached. She wanted him deep inside her. She needed him to fill her and he did.

Deeper and deeper. He controlled her breathing. Leaving her just a little short of air until finally, his huge cock was seated firmly within her, her nose buried in his pelvis. Then he pushed just a little more, deep into her throat, filling her with his hard warmth.

Only Talcor's hands on her head kept her upright. He moved back and forth before withdrawing nearly out of her mouth. She gulped a quick breath as he moved forward again, slowly but relentlessly. Her jaw ached, her throat burned, yet she longed for him to go even deeper.

She tried to move forward to hurry the penetration but Talcor held her head firmly in place as he controlled the depth and speed of his relentless motion. In and out, taunting her with his control. Time passed without meaning until finally Shelley screamed around his cock as he exploded deep into her throat while her pelvis clenched impossibly tight before exploding into a wave of release that shook her very depths.

The climax left her weak and when Talcor pulled back and freed her, she slumped to the floor, unable to stay upright against the waves of pleasure.

Focused inward on the sensations filling her, she started when Talcor swept her off the floor. "Don't relax. We are not done yet. You are mine. You will do as I say. You will obey me and I think you need one more lesson," he said as he carried her down the hallway.

Shelley couldn't prevent the stray thought that she'd quite enjoyed the last lesson as she cuddled into Talcor's warmth.

Drowsy and not paying attention to her surroundings, Shelley was unprepared when Talcor dropped her to her feet and grabbed both wrists, pulling her arms high over her head.

"You'll wait here until I say otherwise," he said, pressing her back against the cold wall and fastening cold steel around her wrists, forcing her to stretch to stand.

Shocked by the sudden change in temperature, from Talcor's warmth to the cold dungeon, Shelley cried, "I'm cold! You can't leave me here like this!"

Talcor grabbed her chin and lifted until Shelley met his eyes. Ice chips seemed to float within them.

"You'll accept anything I chose to do to you."

"No...please—"

"Quiet!" Talcor paused, eyes narrowing. "Or perhaps you'd prefer I blindfold and gag you?"

She felt male strength, barely leashed. Strength aimed at controlling her. Her feminine parts exulted that she could drive a man to such a point while her mind screamed at her that she was in serious danger.

"I can break you," Talcor whispered into Shelley's ear.

"Do you want to?" she asked, closing her eyes, trying to relax into his strength. His statement wasn't an idle claim, she couldn't fight him physically. All she had were her wits.

Talcor wrapped his arms around her. They tightened infinitesimally and Shelley felt the pressure against her ribs. Her breathing was so shallow now that she felt lightheaded and for the first time she wondered if he'd really hurt her, permanently damage her, not just play a game.

Concentrating on breathing and controlling her fear, she was unprepared for Talcor's next question. "Have you ever felt pain inflicted by a trusted partner?" Images of the things he'd done to Pella flooded her mind.

His arms tightened a little more. "Answer me. Have you?"

"Isn't that what you did to me last night?"

"Ah, you trust me?"

Shelley froze as realization slammed into her consciousness. She did trust him. Despite everything, she did trust him. "No," she whispered.

"You lie," Talcor stated. "You lie to me. You lie to yourself. Answer truthfully. Do you want to play games that include pain?"

"With you, you mean?" Shelley asked, trying to stall. She wasn't sure she wanted to answer that question or even if she could answer it. She had no way to judge. Could she willingly accept Talcor's invitation? He was far different from the partners she'd had previously. He'd stay in control. She'd have little option but to take what he gave.

"Shelley, I am the only partner you will ever have. Of course I mean with me. Do you want me to teach you the value of pain mixed with pleasure until you aren't sure which is which and you never want it to end?"

Shelley swallowed hard, stunned by Talcor's sudden inflexibility and cruelty. She bit her lip to stop the rush of words threatening to explode.

Smiling, Talcor said, "Much better. Just one last thing…"

Shelley's arms were already aching. What else could he do to her? He wasn't seriously going to leave her hanging here, was he? Why was he so angry?

She watched him move to a cabinet and rummage in it for a few moments. His back blocked her view and she couldn't see what he picked up, even though she heard his exclamation of satisfaction. What was in his hand? Whatever it was, he kept it well hidden as he walked back to her.

Shelley's heart raced at the sight of his face. He was definitely pleased.

"Cold?" he asked gently, stroking her left nipple. "Or aroused?" He continued stroking before bending to lick it, encouraging it to grow larger and sending arrows of need into her cunt.

Shelley's breath hitched and she clenched her thighs. How could he arouse her so much with such gentle touches? She rested her head back against the cold stone, sinking into the incredible sensations coursing through her. She wished he'd work on her other breast too but she knew better than to ask.

Lost in sensation, Shelley screamed when a sharp, painful bite suddenly gripped her aroused nipple. Looking down, she saw a vicious-looking clamp, its teeth buried deep, flattening her nipple. Waves of agony coursed up her nipple to her arm. She gasped for breath, "Please…"

"Yes, you need its mate, don't you?"

Shelley's eyes widened in horror. She tried to squirm away as Talcor turned his attention to her right nipple. She writhed, trying to free herself from the nipple clamp as Talcor sent waves of need coursing through her body. She moaned. Pain and pleasure mingled, confusing her senses. Her attention bounced between one breast and the other.

"That's it, feel the pain, feel the pleasure—you can't escape either. I say what you feel and when you feel it," Talcor murmured before placing the second clamp.

Shelley couldn't stop the scream that escaped.

Talcor pressed into her body, pushing her against the cold stone, his hard chest flattening her breasts, creating an even deeper bite of the clamps. "You will stay here until released. Think about the clamps, think about the pain. If you are good, you'll be able to sink into it and ride the pain. If you aren't good it will just hurt. Your choice. Either way you will learn not to fight me."

Talcor stepped back and took one last look before leaving the dungeon and locking the door behind him.

Shelley, tears streaming down her face, just looked at the closed door. She couldn't believe he'd left her like this. Her breasts ached. Underneath the ache though was an insidious thread of arousal. She could still feel the device from last night and her subsequent orgasm. She could feel moisture dripping down from her cunt. Did she like this? She shook her head. She was too confused to make sense of it all. For now she'd just try to survive until she gained her freedom.

Chapter Eleven

ℬ

Pella, come to the library. Come to me now.

Pella felt Talcor's call through their link. He still seemed angry. Pella frowned, upset by Talcor's anger. She knew it wasn't aimed only at her, but in all her years with him, it was the first time the anger seemed to control him. Pella rubbed the arm he'd grabbed earlier. He'd never hurt her in anger before. Was Shelley pushing him past his limits? If so, that wasn't a good thing and his anger boded no good for her request. She sighed as she descended the stairway. She hoped he wasn't beyond rationality.

Pella reached the library and stood waiting in the doorway. "Master?" she said.

Talcor looked up. He waved his hand for her to enter the room. "It is time for us to talk." He paused then said, "Talk to me."

Pella stood silent for a moment, her head bowed. She took a deep breath and raised her head. Meeting Talcor's glance, she said, "Is this woman the one for you?"

"Perhaps, but it is not your place to question. We're here to discuss our link—our damaged link."

Pella stood defiant, meeting Talcor's stare with one of her own. Then she took another deep breath, and said, "If she's the one for you, we are no longer. I've seen the way you look at her. I've felt your desire."

"Does the possibility hurt you?"

"No, you know better than that. We've known since the start that our link was not strong enough to go further. She is the one for you."

Talcor frowned. "She's an off-worlder. I have no desire to bond with a woman who doesn't understand or respect our culture."

A quick smile crossed her face. "Is that why you're angry? You know the magic of the bonding doesn't always respect our wishes."

Talcor cocked an eyebrow. "Obviously. I felt your joy last night. I felt you repudiate our bond."

"I am sorry, Master, I couldn't stop myself. Will you finish freeing me?"

"Are you certain that is your wish?"

"You know you can't go further with Shelley without freeing me."

"That's not an answer. You have to say it. Pella, do you want your freedom?"

She didn't answer. Instead, she moved to the window that overlooked Talcor's gardens. The lilacs were in their last bloom and the rich, warm scent carried the promise of summer.

Talcor stood and moved behind her. Placing his hands on her shoulders, he leaned forward and noticed her eyes glistening with unshed tears. "Pella? What's happened with that weakling Jared?"

She took in another deep breath. "I did as you asked and satisfied the man."

"Was it very bad? I would not have you harmed, you know that."

A quick laugh escaped before she sobered, and whispered, "Quite the opposite. He's not weak...just different. Different from any other man I've ever met."

"Pella?"

"I think — no, I know — he and I are fated to link...but, he doesn't know how to link us. He doesn't know about the words." Shuddering, she closed her eyes and took a deep breath. When she spoke, her words rushed out. "I told him what I know. Will you free me from my bond to you, teach him the words and teach him how to complete the ritual? I trust the magic. I'd prefer you explained to Jared but I won't be stopped." She shook her head. "We can't stop."

Talcor realized the same strength that had coursed through her veins during their games filled her now.

Her request shocked Talcor. Even though he'd felt her happiness with Jared last night, he hadn't really considered that it might be a true linking. Given Marissa's response to Kytar and Shelley's response to him, he knew bonding with off-worlders was possible, something no Darinthian had really considered before. It was an understood custom that only Darinthians could complete the ritual binding. He definitely hadn't expected any Darinthian woman to seek a bond with an outside male. A twinge of jealousy sparked and then died.

While he and Pella had been together for years, the bonds had never tightened and he'd never felt the urge to collar her, to make their companionship permanent. Without his collar, nothing stopped her from requesting her freedom. And they'd both known it would end some day. But he'd never thought she'd request her freedom only to give it to an off-worlder.

As the silence grew, Pella arched her head and looked up at Talcor. "I did not expect this either," she said with a sad half smile. "I've been happy here but we both know our link is not strong. It was always merely comfortable."

"The off-worlder will eventually leave Darinth. What happens then?"

She shook her head and looked back out on the garden. She whispered, "I don't know. I just know I long for him to say the words. I need him to say the words," she said with a defiant tilt to her head.

Talcor had never seen Pella so assertive. For a brief instant he considered refusal, though he knew it would benefit neither of them. Talcor closed his eyes. A vision of Shelley flashed into his mind.

Sighing, he kissed Pella's head and said, "I will free you. You're right. I have to free you because Shelley is the one for me."

"I know." Pella smiled. "You've never hurt me in anger before. She must be something if she can drive you to lose control."

Talcor closed his eyes. "I'm sorry—"

"No! Don't apologize, just recognize your limits."

Talcor met her gaze. "How did you get so wise?" Not waiting for an answer, he smiled, and whispered, "Pella, I repudiate our bond and set you free."

A shudder echoed from Talcor to Pella as the final link in their bond broke and separated, leaving them two individuals locked in a hug but separate in every other way. They looked at each other, feeling a brief twinge of regret at the parting of their ways.

"It is done. You are free, though I'd prefer you didn't leave until I've spoken with Jared. I need to satisfy myself that he can and will take care of you. You have the shelter of my home for as long as is necessary."

"Shelley won't like that."

"Your safety is not subject to her whims. You're a valuable and cherished friend. I will see you safe."

Pella smiled and leaned back against Talcor's chest. "Thank you, Master."

"No, not Master, just Talcor," he replied softly. "Our bond is broken. You are free."

"As are you," she replied.

He nodded and released her. "Send Jared to me."

"Please treat him gently. He didn't know—doesn't know and doesn't understand."

Talcor swatted Pella's rear. "Get him. He and I will discuss what's necessary."

Pella turned toward the door.

"Oh and, Pella, one last favor?"

She turned and looked at him.

"Shelley is chained in the dungeon. After you send Jared to me, go to her. Maybe you can talk some sense into her. I don't trust myself near her right now."

"Talk? Is that all you want me to do?"

Talcor drew in a deep breath. "You find her attractive?"

Pella shrugged. "Maybe. She has a lot of fire…but I'm certain Jared would not forgive me if I played games with Shelley. I'm not certain you would either."

"You're right. Just talk to her. When you're done, release the nipple clamps and unchain her. Help her to her bedroom. "

Pella nodded and went to find Jared.

Talcor walked to the bar. He poured a drink and tossed it back.

With Shelley's resistance and the demands of the bond, he felt off balance and conflicted. Where was his vaunted control? He felt buffeted by a tempest he could only ride out.

He'd known he would have to set Pella free before completing the ritual with Shelley. A man was not permitted to complete the ritual with another while he still had a first-stage companion. He hadn't expected Pella to ask for her freedom first though. Another slight twinge of jealously flared through him before he chuckled. The magic easily made a man a fool. Kytar hadn't warned him of that fact but it explained much about Kytar's actions.

Talcor had known since the first moment he saw Shelley that she belonged with him as his bonded companion. Nothing stood in the way now. Nothing stopped him from taking the next step with Shelley. *Nothing except Shelley*, he thought with grim determination.

* * * * *

Pella found Jared reading a book in his bedroom. He stood and met her in the middle of the room, gently caressing her cheek and pulling her close before softly kissing her.

Pella pulled back. Meeting his eyes, she said, "Jared, Talcor wants to talk to you. He's in the library."

Jared looked at Pella's serious face. "Talk to me about what? He's not angry at me, is he? He doesn't want to kill me, does he?"

"No, nothing like that," she replied, shaking her head.

"Then what?"

"He wants to talk to you about..."

"About what?"

"About Darinthian magic," she replied with a defiant toss of her head.

Jared shook his head. "I don't believe in your magic," Jared stated with conviction.

"Did you feel nothing last night? Didn't you feel that we belonged together? Together in a way you've never felt with any other woman?"

"You know I did. You know I didn't want to stop. You know I want to make you mine. Explain to me how I can do that."

"I can't explain, only another male may do that. I've spoken with Talcor. That's why he wants to talk to you."

Jared took a step back from Pella. He frowned and remained silent.

"Talcor is worried about my safety. He's released me. I'm no longer his companion but you don't know how to complete our link. It is dangerous for me to be free."

"Released you? That sounds barbaric and what do you mean dangerous? As if I could ever hurt you!"

"Well, that is part of the problem," Pella said with a laugh in her voice. "I'm used to being hurt."

"You can't really like that, can you?"

Pella's eyes twinkled. "It does have its attractions. We can deal with that issue later. Right now you have to go talk to him."

"I'd rather not."

"Then we'll never be together," she countered.

"But I don't believe in your magic."

"Oh no? How did you feel when I entered the room? How do you feel right now?"

"Excited to see you. I need you."

"Yes." She smiled. "Just as I need you. That's the magic telling us we belong together."

"Not just hormones?"

"No, not here on Darinth. Oh, go talk to Talcor. He'll explain it better than I can."

Jared moved closer, and said, "Only for you will I do this. If it were up to me, I'd put the whole planet between Talcor and me." He kissed her and left the room.

Pella stood for a moment before sighing and going to keep her promise to Talcor.

* * * * *

Shelley's arms ached. She longed to sit down, to release the pressure on her wrists. The bindings weren't too tight but she had to stand on tiptoe, otherwise her arms took all her weight. How long was he going to leave her hanging there like a slab of meat?

It even felt like a meat locker in the dungeon. The stones at her back were cold and the cold slowly crept into her bones. She shivered, her nipples taut with a mixture of cold and need.

The clamps bit deep, numbing even while arousing her. She squirmed and felt a trace of moisture drip down her thighs.

She was angry and aroused, which simply made her angrier. She'd never imagined that being helpless could be so freeing. She didn't have to worry about anything. She didn't have to think about anything. She wasn't going anywhere until Talcor decided to release her. If only she didn't ache so much. The worst part was that the ache wasn't just from physical discomfort. She was aroused and her pussy ached with emptiness.

"It is one of Talcor's favorite games. How long do you think you'll last?"

Shelley stiffened. She didn't need the reminder that this twit had been with Talcor and she certainly didn't want Pella to see her so helpless. Her embarrassment made her spit out the question, "Last until what?"

"Last until you pass out," Pella replied.

Shelley stared at her. She hadn't really considered that Talcor might just leave her here.

Pella cocked her head. "Do you want to get free?"

"Yes!"

Pella smiled. "Why? Don't you like Talcor? Don't you feel the connection?" she asked, moving close. Shelley stared at the diminutive woman, not certain she wanted to answer Pella's questions.

Pella laughed. "Never mind. I don't think you know how to be honest with yourself, much less with me. Talcor is a wonderful companion. You are a fool to continue your senseless defiance. You can't win against him. Besides, if you gained your freedom, you'd lose a fantastic lover. How would that be winning?" asked Pella.

"I'm an independent woman. I'm not like you. I'm not a man's toy! I saw your vid. I saw how weak you are," spit out Shelley.

"No man's toy? Really? Do you think Talcor would agree?"

Shelley ignored Pella's question.

Stepping away from Shelley, Pella sighed. "Talking to you is pointless. Do you want me to free you and help you to your bedroom?"

Shelley glared at Pella.

Pella shrugged. "Answer me or you can stay here, chained and clamped."

Shelley's heart raced. She wanted to tell Pella to go to hell, but by the expression on Pella's face, she was serious. She was quite capable of walking out and leaving Shelley cold and sore. Shelley bit down her anger and nodded. "Help me."

"Say please."

Shelley glared at the small woman, but said, "Please help me."

Pella smiled and reached out to flick off one clamp then the other. Shelley nearly screamed as the blood flowed back into her nipples. The pain was brief but intensely agonizing.

Pella stood silently watching Shelley struggle to regain her breath.

"Help me down," Shelley demanded as soon as she was able.

Pella arched an eyebrow.

"Please help me down."

Pella reached out and pressed a button, releasing the chains.

Shelley nearly stumbled as her feet took her weight. She hadn't realized how debilitating standing on tiptoe could be.

Pella quickly unfastened the wrist restraints and threw a robe at Shelley.

Another companion robe Shelley realized. She longed to throw it to the floor but that would be stupid. Shelley was cold, sore and just a little weak. She just wanted the safety of her bedroom. Illusory safety, she knew, but at least away from Pella and Talcor. She took a step. Her knees buckled and only Pella's quick action saved her from a fall.

"Let me help," said Pella as she put an arm around Shelley's waist.

Shelley acquiesced because she had no choice. She and Pella slowly made their way upstairs. As Pella left her at the door to her room, Shelley unbent enough to say, "Thank you."

Pella laughed. "Don't thank me. Talcor asked me to free you. Nothing in this house happens without his approval. You'd do well to learn that fact."

Shelley stiffened and slammed the door on Pella's laughter and made her way to the bathroom. She needed a nice hot relaxing bath.

* * * * *

Jared entered the library, eyeing Talcor warily. He didn't trust the man and he had to admit that he was just a little—no, a lot—intimidated by him. He hoped Talcor wasn't going to berate him for enjoying Pella's favors. After all, Pella was Talcor's companion too and he had made it very clear that Shelley wasn't to be touched. Maybe Jared had misunderstood. Maybe Pella was off limits too. But Talcor didn't look angry as he handed Jared a drink and waved him to a chair.

Talcor frowned down at his drink. Then he raised his head and pinned Jared to his seat. "Darinth's sexual practices are misunderstood by the rest of the galaxy. We do not correct this misunderstanding because our sexual practices are sacred. They are not fodder for gossip. I am about to tell you some of our practices. I hope you will honor the trust I give you."

Jared stared at Talcor, wondering if he should tell him that Pella had already told him about Darinthian customs. Deciding to remain silent about that, he said, "Just tell me how to make her mine."

"It isn't that simple. I know Pella talked to you but Pella doesn't know everything. She sees only the female side. You need to know the male side. Pella has asked me to do this. I have agreed. Will you honor the trust I give you if I explain our customs?"

"Of course I will."

Talcor closed his eyes and gave a short nod. "Very well." He took another drink before setting aside his glass and leaning forward.

"Some of the things I tell you, Pella may have mentioned but you will listen. Some of the things I tell you will shock you. Just remember our customs have developed over thousands of years. The first thing you should know is that there is magic on Darinth."

"So Pella told me but there's no such thing as magic," Jared exclaimed.

"No? Then why was Shelley affected by my words in the arrival center? Why do you long for a woman you've just met? A longing that goes far beyond physical lust?"

Jared had no answer. He leaned back in his chair, trying to wrap his head around the fact that Darinthians might actually have access to magic.

"Thousands of years ago, Darinth was a barbaric planet." He held up his hand as if to intercept a protest from Jared. "I know there are those who say it is still barbaric but it is not, not like it was long ago. Numerous predators roamed the planet and multiple dangers existed. Men were strong enough to deal with the dangers, women weren't. Yet women were essential to our survival as a species. A system developed to protect our women. Under that system, any male would die to protect a bonded woman."

"Bonded. Still sounds barbaric."

"It's not. Bonding is something like your marriage. A woman who is not bonded is fair game for any man. Our women are happy in bondage because it means a man cares enough to protect them. Without the bonding, they'd be prey for any man, a dangerous position, as Shelley found out. The first stage, what I have done to Shelley, is like an engagement."

"But Pella said it was like dating…"

Talcor glared at Jared. "Dating, an engagement, those are your terms, not ours. It can be either or neither or something else altogether. Binding is a commitment but it is a commitment that can be undone if both agree. A good thing for you and Pella, don't you agree?" Talcor asked.

His voice sent shivers down Jared's spine. Jared nodded but remained silent.

Talcor continued. "The claiming words, the words I said to Shelley are magic. When they are said to a woman, a bond link is created between the man and woman. I always know where Shelley is, I can feel her in a part of my head and she can feel me though she doesn't realize exactly what she's feeling," he said, smiling. "Whether you believe in magic or not, this is reality on Darinth."

"But you've claimed both Shelley and Pella. On my world, you wouldn't be engaged to two women."

"I said bonding was similar, I didn't say it was the same. In the first stage, I may claim as many women as I feel able to protect because that's what bonding is, it is a promise of protection and the first stage of companionship. Every Darinthian male on the planet recognizes another's claim and will honor it."

"You mean…" Jared stopped, feeling a little stunned. "You mean that men know whether a woman is claimed or not?"

"Yes. That's why Shelley was in danger in the arrival area. Every Darinthian man knew she wasn't claimed. It's an imperative for us. None of us wanted to leave her unclaimed. She was in danger. Every man wanted to claim her to protect her."

"You're saying that any Darinthian male will protect Shelley now?"

"Exactly."

"Does she know this?"

"No," Talcor snorted. "She doesn't want to know."

Jared grinned. "That's Shelley."

Talcor waved his hand, dismissing the subject. "I didn't bring you here to discuss my companion."

"Why did you bring me here? You haven't told me how to claim Pella yet."

"I know Pella wants to be your companion."

"Uhh…how do you feel about that?"

"Pella and I have been together a long time but we both knew our bonds would never tighten."

"Tighten?"

"The second and final stage of companionship is collaring. A female accepts a male's collar and he says the claiming words."

"Collar? That's really barbaric symbolism. Shelley will pitch a fit about that."

"We're not here to discuss Shelley. We're discussing Pella. She and I have always known that one day our relationship would end. I would have her happy. She thinks you're the one to collar her."

"Okay…then after the collar, then what, you're married?"

"You may call it that, though it goes far beyond marriage and it is permanent."

"Far beyond how?"

"We will not discuss that, at least not now."

"How do you and Pella know your relationship won't go further?"

Talcor sighed, he really didn't want to explain but he knew he must for Pella's sake. "When the binding words are first spoken a link snaps into place. If the pair is meant to be together, the linking is an intense experience. We feel how far we may go. Pella and I will go no further."

"And you'll give her up, just like that?" Jared asked, remembering Talcor's jealousy in the arrival center.

"I have already given her up. Our bond is broken but I will let her leave this house only if I know she will be protected by another."

Suddenly Jared realized where Talcor was heading with this conversation. His heart soared at the thought of claiming Pella for his own, of having her with him always. "You've released her to me…" he sighed out, hardly daring to believe that Talcor could give Pella up.

"Only if you promise to bind her while you are here."

"And when I leave, will she come with me?"

Talcor leaned back in his chair. "Do you want that?"

"Oh yes, I want that very much," Jared stated without hesitation.

"I know of no other bonded pair who lives off Darinth. There is no precedent. I don't know if the magic will work off-planet. Although I think Shelley and I made a connection before she arrived on Darinth, so there is a possibility."

"With or without magic, I will take care of her. She is mine," Jared spit out before he thought about his words. He expected Talcor's anger and wasn't prepared for his laughter.

"Perhaps Pella is right. Perhaps you are meant to be together. I cannot make this decision myself. I know of no other off-world man who has been initiated into Darinthian customs."

"I thought you were going to explain how I bind Pella."

"First I wanted to determine your commitment. I wanted to make sure you didn't just see Pella as a convenience. I can't initiate you before I consult with an elder. I'll do so tomorrow. In the meantime, enjoy her company but not her favors."

Jared sighed and left the library. As he trudged up the stairs, he wondered how he would survive another day without having sex with Pella. He didn't want to wait but he knew he had no choice. He now had a better understanding of the necessity of waiting. One more day and she'd be his forever. He wouldn't risk losing her. He could wait.

* * * * *

Later that evening, though it was late and Talcor knew he should leave Shelley to her thoughts and needs, he couldn't resist seeing her. His heart ached when they weren't close and he could feel her need for sex.

He chuckled as he went looking for Shelley. Wouldn't she be furious if she knew just how much of her emotions were bared to him. She wasn't in her bedroom or the kitchen or dining area or any other room he might have expected. He wasn't worried. He knew she was still in the house. He could feel her. He was startled though when he realized there was only one place left to look.

The dungeon door was cracked open. He peeked inside and saw Shelley running her hands over his selection of whips and crops, a dreamy look on her face. Her need beat at him. The whips and crops aroused her to a fevered peak.

He wouldn't have thought she'd admit her desires, even to herself. Clearly he was wrong. For once she wasn't raging or yelling or arguing with him. He wanted to capture her present mood and treasure it. *Soon*, he told himself. Soon she'd capitulate and accept her position. She had to. He wouldn't be responsible for his anger if she didn't.

He hesitated in the doorway. Perhaps he should just leave her to her yearnings. No, he decided, the magic wouldn't let him leave his companion in such a needy state. He sighed, trying to work out how to satisfy her without making things worse. Perhaps it was time for the collar. He was free of Pella and Shelley had already agreed. A quick collaring and binding was what he needed and if he could only ignore her needs, they'd be bound by morning.

Chapter Twelve

෨

Shelley started when she heard the snick of the lock. Talcor stood with the door at his back. She felt like a trapped animal. She hadn't expected Talcor to seek her out so late and how embarrassing it was for him to find her here in his lair, mooning over the crop, remembering what he'd done to Pella and imagining what it felt like.

As if sensing her panic, Talcor held out a hand. "I am very pleased to find you here. I wasn't sure you'd willingly come back after your earlier session."

Shelley tossed her head. "I'm not afraid of you," she said even as she silently cursed her stupidity for coming back to this room.

Talcor paused, ignoring her statement. Instead he said, "You're curious. Would you like a taste of them?" he asked, waving toward the whips. "Just a small taste, not a full session. You're not ready for that."

As if Talcor had sucked all the air out of the chamber, Shelley's throat closed. She wanted to scream, *No!* She wanted to deny her need. She wanted to fight him. Instead, she looked at him, helplessly not able to say "no", not able to say "yes". What was happening to her?

Talcor moved forward slowly until he stood beside her. He touched a strand of hair. Moving it out of the way and kissing the side of her throat, he lifted her into his arms. Carrying her to the wall, he whispered, "Let's just play a little. It is senseless to deny your need."

Quickly stripping off her robe and sandals, he held her wrists in one hand and pulled her arms high. Reaching up with his other hand, he wound the restraint tight and pulled until Shelley was on her toes, off balance and held upright only by Talcor's body pressing her into the cold stone wall. Bare skin was no protection against the cold. Remembering her earlier session, her nipples tightened and she shivered.

Shelley wanted to scream her refusal but she couldn't get the words past the lump in her throat. Talcor's confident, soft actions hadn't frightened her, she realized as she felt moisture dripping down her thighs. His powerful arms made her feel safe and protected, even as her lust increased. The throbbing need in her pussy stopped her from saying anything. She didn't know what to say. No man had ever treated her like this. One minute he was demanding and abrasive, the next soft and gentle. It was as if Talcor knew her fantasies and was determined to bring them to life.

Shelley closed her eyes when Talcor took a nipple between two fingers. Still bruised from her earlier session in the clamps, she gasped at the sensation. Not painful exactly but definitely achy.

Talcor took no notice of her gasp as he rolled the beaded nub with a gentle pressure that gradually intensified, becoming nearly painful then pushing beyond pain. Holding her nipple erect, he bent his head until his mouth could capture the delicate bead. Once more he started gently but didn't stop, and as the pressure increased, Shelley realized he was marking her breast. The hickey should have been painful but instead it was the most arousing thing she'd ever felt. By starting soft and increasing the pressure, he'd accustomed her to a pain she wouldn't have tolerated if he'd started with the pain first.

He raised his head, and said, "Look at my mark."

Shelley looked down to see a perfect red circle surrounding her nipple. Her gut tightened and she nearly begged him to satisfy her, to take her in any way he chose. She felt his chuckle deep in his chest as he started on the other nipple.

Shelley moaned. She didn't know if she could survive a second marking but she was eager to find out. He pinched harder this time and her senses wavered, not certain if it was pain or pleasure she felt. She longed to move a hand to touch his hair as he lowered his head a second time and drew her deeply into his mouth.

After finishing the second mark, he raised his head, and said, "Look at yourself. You belong to me. You've agreed to accept my collar and I want to see it around your throat."

She moaned as he deliberately increased the pressure of his strokes. Now gently circling her nipples, never quite touching them, they grew like flowers seeking the sunlight. She moaned, longing to scream with need but unable to give it voice. Still he didn't touch her nipples this time.

Talcor's hand circled her neck. "Your neck is bare without my collar." He tightened his hand a little, not enough to choke her, just enough so she felt him when she tried to swallow the lump in her throat. His fingers moved in a tender stroke, followed by his tongue as he held her still. His mouth fastened on the spot where her neck met her shoulder and she shivered as he sucked the blood to the surface.

Finishing the third mark he trailed back up to just below her earlobe and place a fourth mark. "Deny me all you wish. I will mark every inch of your body until you are mindless with need. I enjoy seeing my marks on your ivory skin. And once I am done marking you," he whispered into her ear, "we will go in public. You'll be naked and on your knees so every male will know my power over you."

Shelley tried to shake her head but a strange lethargy took hold of her senses. His words inflamed her blood, causing it to rush through her veins like molten heat until it reached her cunt and pooled in a relentless grip of need. Her arms ached from being raised so high and her feet started to cramp but the pain/pleasure of her nipples caused all other thoughts to flee. She'd never felt so helpless. She'd never felt so aroused.

Talcor tilted her head to the other side. She lost track of how many marks he placed. Her eyes half closed, she moaned as his determined assault took every bit of her will. She tried to squirm to ease the relentless ache in her pelvis but Talcor held her motionless.

"Take me," she finally moaned, unable to stand any more, her desire at fever pitch, unlike anything she'd ever felt before.

"Are you ready? Do you want the whip or the crop?" Talcor paused to look at Shelley's flushed face and wild eyes. "Do you want me to decide?"

"No! No whipping. I need release."

Talcor moved close, pressing her against the cold wall. "I'll decide what you need and when you need it. Shelley, you keep forgetting your place," he whispered.

"Then please just do something. I don't think I can last much longer."

"You'll last as long as I say," Talcor said, reaching back and selecting a flail with numerous wide leather strips. He trailed it over Shelley's shoulders and breasts.

The strands were incredibly soft as they caressed her skin. Shelley wondered how anything so soft could be at all painful.

Reaching out, Talcor twisted the chain holding Shelley, moving her so she faced the wall, her sensitive nipples pressed into the cold stone.

The first slash caught her by surprise. She learned the soft strands turned into sharp, stinging lines when wielded at speed. That sensation was followed immediately by a warm hand caressing her butt, massaging away the pain. Talcor repeated the pattern again and yet again. Pain then soft pleasure until he stopped the pattern and struck her five times in quick succession. Shelley's cunt clenched with need, confused by the pain, feeling as though it were pleasure. Talcor pressed close behind her and reached down to finger her clit. Softly then with increasing pressure.

"Don't come yet, Shelley," he whispered in her ear.

The pressure increased until Shelley screamed for release. Drenched in sweat, unable to stand, she leaned back against Talcor's broad chest. She knew he wasn't going to penetrate her with his cock. She felt tight with need. How much longer could he drag this out? Much as she might hate her current position, she couldn't deny Talcor's ability. The man knew his way around a woman's body. She relented and begged, "Please…please…finish it!"

"No," he replied, "not until you willingly ask for my collar."

"I've already agreed to the collar!"

"Yes, but you haven't accepted the inevitability of it. And you really don't want it. I won't be satisfied and neither will you until you're willingly wearing my collar." He moved a finger to her slit and started tapping on her clitoris.

Shelley's head lolled back as she moved toward the peak but again he stopped before she could fall over it.

"Don't stop…please don't stop," she begged.

"It is time to finish this. Beg for my collar!"

"I can't," she screamed at him, angry that he would keep her on this never-ending peak without sending her over the edge.

"You can. You must if you ever want to come again. Don't think I don't know about all the masturbation you've done when you thought you were alone in your room. You won't have another orgasm until you are collared."

Embarrassment warred with arousal. How did he know about that? Would he really stop her? She wanted to deny his power but knew she couldn't. Wasn't he in the process of proving that she couldn't fight him?

Talcor slipped two fingers into her dripping pussy. Shelley clenched her muscles, trying to hold him there long enough for completion but his fingers slid out before she could finish. Again and again, he proved his power over her until she groaned, "Enough, I can't stand any more."

"You know what I want," he whispered in her ear.

"No," Shelley moaned.

"Then suffer," he said, moving away from her.

Feeling weak, she sagged against the pull of the chains. "Don't leave me like this!"

"Maybe if you spend the night like this, you'll be more cooperative. Pella won't free you this time."

Shelley startled. "No, please…"

Talcor's eyes narrowed. "If I unchain you, you must promise not to masturbate."

Her eyes widened.

"Oh yes, I felt your masturbation. You've had a good time, haven't you?" he asked while flicking a nipple. "No more. No more satisfaction until you surrender to me."

"Talcor—"

"Do you promise not to masturbate?" Before she could answer, he placed a finger on her lips. "Be careful! I'll know if you lie."

Shelley swallowed hard. She didn't quite believe he'd know but she didn't want to take that risk. "I promise."

Talcor smiled and swatted her bruised ass. It was all Shelley could do to remain standing against the wave of pain and longing that poured through her body. Then he reached up and unchained her. Sweeping her into his arms and holding her tightly, he climbed the stairs to her bedroom and put her to bed.

* * * * *

Shelley woke in a foul mood. She'd spent most of the night in a state of sexual frustration. Her sore nipples and bruised ass contributed to her arousal. An arousal she hadn't satisfied. She hadn't been quite brave enough to defy Talcor's command not to masturbate. Besides, it was embarrassing to think he might actually be able to read her emotions and tell when she had an orgasm. She sighed and got out of bed. After taking a shower, she dressed and headed for the dining room.

Talcor was eating breakfast, his back to the doorway.

Shelley hesitated, debating whether to come back later, but before she could move away, Talcor turned his head and motioned her into the room.

Standing, he said, "Come and eat! I'll let you satisfy that need at least."

Shelley's face flamed. He had to be guessing. He couldn't really read her emotions, could he?

Talcor laughed. "Yes, I can read your emotions and it is good you didn't defy me and satisfy yourself. I'll leave now so you can eat in peace."

Shelley, angered by his amusement, forgot her fear of this man, and said, "You can't keep me here! I have to get back to work!"

"Are you back to your senseless demands? You should have thought about the dangers before you traveled to Darinth. You were warned," Talcor replied. "Besides, you falsely claim we've kidnapped Marissa and brainwashed her. So now you will stay here until she can speak to you. I'm fairly certain Kytar will give his permission. Be happy that I'll allow it. I don't have to let you ever see anyone." He paused and his eyes grew colder. "If you do not behave, I can withdraw my permission. The hospitality of my house is yours. Pella will see to your needs. In the meantime, I have duties that require my presence elsewhere."

"No!"

Talcor turned from the door, his eyebrows raised. "You wish me to stay?"

"If you leave, I'll find Marissa on my own."

"And how will you do that? If you step foot outside this house without me, any Darinthian male may hold you until I return. Make no mistake. No Darinthian male will help you in any way. They will protect you whether you wish it or not but

I doubt they will be as understanding as I've been. You talked to Davo. You talked to the ambassador. Do you really need more proof that you must wait?"

"I won't just sit here and do nothing. I can't."

Talcor's eyes narrowed. His voice was dangerously soft as he said, "Perhaps I should chain you so I know you will be safe."

Shelley just glared at him. Green eyes flashing with anger. "Is this what happened to Marissa? Did some Darinthian male decide she needed protection, whether she wanted it or not?"

Talcor's lips curled into a grin. "As a matter of fact, that is exactly what happened."

"Then she's been kidnapped just like I have!" Shelley screamed.

Talcor frowned. "I have an errand. We'll continue this discussion when I return," he said before exiting the room, leaving Shelley fuming.

Shelley nibbled on some fruit while she stomped around the room, trying to work off her excess energy. She was determined to figure out how to see Marissa then how to get off this forsaken planet. To get away from Talcor and his continual demands. Her response to him terrified her. Where was her vaunted independence?

Shelley looked up to see Jared in the doorway. "Jared, you have to help me find Marissa and get off this planet!"

"Shelley —"

"No," she interrupted, "Talcor has left. We just need to walk out there and find Marissa."

"Shelley, haven't you learned anything? We can't leave the house. You wouldn't be safe. And even if we did leave, how are we going to find Marissa? She could be anywhere. You're not making sense."

"Have you let that little twit convince you that this society is okay?"

Jared stiffened. "That little twit's name is Pella and we've fallen in love."

"You've what?" Shelley screamed. "How could you?"

Pella rushed into the room. "Why are you screaming? What's going on?"

Shelley felt her face flush with heat. She didn't want to believe Pella was genuinely nice and she couldn't—she wouldn't—forgive Pella for seeing her in a weakened state yesterday.

Pella moved to stand next to Jared, circling his waist with her arm and pressing close, ignoring Shelley's glare. "What's going on?"

Jared smiled down at Pella and placed a soft kiss on her head. "Good morning. Shelley is just being Shelley. Nothing serious."

Shelley fumed. "How can you say that," she started to protest. Jared and Pella ignored her, intertwined and obviously fixated on each other. Shelley, disgusted by the display said, "Oh get a room already."

Jared pulled his gaze from Pella, "Not until we're bound."

"Bound?" asked Shelley. "What are you talking about?"

Jared grinned. "I've been touched by the magic. Talcor's started my lessons but he said he couldn't finish until he'd talked to an elder. Then I'll be able to bind Pella as my companion."

"You're touched all right. You can't seriously buy into this stuff!"

"Jealous, Shelley?" interrupted Pella. "But who are you jealous of? Jared or me?"

Shelley's face flamed.

Jared frowned. "Pella, what are you talking about?"

"Shelley doesn't like me because she saw a vid of Talcor and me. She's jealous," said Pella, moving even closer to Jared.

"This is less about Shelley's concern for you than her dislike of me."

"That's nonsense. It's about my dislike of rape and coercion. Talcor doesn't own me," said Shelley with a defiant toss of her head.

"I feel sorry for you," said Pella. "Darinthian women are born with the knowledge of the binding. It is not something to fear or hate. We rejoice in it. Remember, the men are bound every bit as much as the women and it can become a binding for life. Darinthian women never have to worry that they'll be tossed out for a younger woman or discarded like an old shoe. We mate for life."

"I will never accept it."

Pella laughed. "You have no choice. It is already too late. You've accepted Talcor's protection and even though he hasn't gone on to the next stage, it is still binding. You could retract your acceptance but I doubt Talcor will allow such a thing. The timing now belongs to Talcor and once the binding is consummated, you will be happy to accept Talcor as your companion."

Uncomfortably aware that Pella might be right, Shelley waved a hand, dismissing Pella's statements. "I have to find Marissa."

"No you don't. Your friend enjoys her captivity. You don't know her very well if you think otherwise," said Pella.

"I don't understand."

Pella cast a pitying look at her. "No...you don't understand. Darinthian women want male protection. We would never dream of denying a male as you are doing. Why would we want to cut ourselves off from our other half?"

"But women shouldn't be slaves! I don't want to wear a collar!"

That startled Pella. "Talcor offered you his collar? Why is your neck still bare? Are you truly so stupid? Do you know how many women have longed to be Talcor's companion? And you throw away the opportunity."

"I won't be any man's slave!"

Pella's laugh tinkled like a mountain brook. "I was a valued companion. To call me a slave is an insult! Men and women are different. We have different strengths. Why would I want to pretend my strength is the same as a male's? Your customs are very bizarre."

"My customs are bizarre?"

"If you'd seen the challenge ritual, you'd know how happy Marissa is!"

"Challenge ritual? What's that? And how did you see it? Was it public?"

Pella cringed away from Shelley's barrage of questions. ""I watched the vid with Talcor. He explained it to me. If you want to see it, you need to watch it with him."

"He's not here and I want to know what's going on. Tell me."

"Shelley, leave Pella alone."

"No!" Shelley said looking at Pella. "Tell me!"

Pella frowned, but she said, "It was such a masterful performance. Marissa was incredible."

"Is the vid here? I want to see it."

Pella shook her head. "Talcor will be back soon. Wait for him. You won't understand it otherwise. You'll get mad and do something foolish."

"Pella, show me the vid," Shelley demanded.

"You might just as well do it," Jared said. "Otherwise, she'll just keep hounding us."

"Talcor won't like it."

"But it will give us time alone," Jared whispered into Pella's ear.

Pella smiled up at him. "If you insist."

Pella led Shelley into the library then searched the shelves until she found the disc she wanted. Starting it, she said, "Shelley, remember this is voluntary. Marissa asked for this." Pella hesitated but Jared took her hand and led her out of the room.

The vid opened with Marissa in bed and two men entering her room.

"Get up," said one of them.

Marissa slowly stood.

"Kneel!" commanded the other man. Shelley started. That was Talcor. Talcor moved so close that his crotch was only millimeters from Marissa's face. He cupped her chin and raised her head. He touched the collar encircling Marissa's throat.

Then the other man moved close behind her. He seized both of her wrists and twisted them harshly behind her, quickly binding her before blindfolding and gagging her.

Shelley's stomach threatened to empty. *Oh Marissa, what have they done to you?* Shelley knew her friend never would have cooperated with these bastards and Talcor was one of them.

In a harsh voice, Talcor ordered Marissa to stand, pulling her when she didn't move fast enough.

The vid cut to a large auditorium filled with men. Shelley watched Marissa walk forward, back straight despite the handicap of the blindfold.

Talcor placed a hand on each shoulder and pushed her down. "Kneel," he commanded in a loud voice.

Once down, they spread Marissa's legs. She lost her balance as she struggled to comply.

Talcor kept his hands on her shoulders.

"Let the ritual begin," said a booming voice.

A different man put a hand between Marissa's shoulder blades and pushed her head to the floor, leaving her bottom high in the air and spread wide open. The man moved around her, circling her. His hand brushed her ass before his arm slashed down. Shelley heard the whistle before she saw the lash and the blooming red line on Marissa's ass.

Shelley rushed from the room, nauseated by Marissa's treatment. She barely made it to her bathroom before losing her breakfast. Leaning back from the toilet, her mind raced. She had to help her friend. Marissa shouldn't be treated like that. She'd be horrified if she knew the public spectacle these monsters had made of her.

Pella came into the bathroom. "I saw you rush upstairs and heard you being sick. What's wrong?"

"What's wrong?" Shelley repeated hysterically. "My friend is being beaten on a public vid! Why would anything be wrong?"

"It is the challenge ritual. Marissa asked for it."

"No woman asks to be beaten like that!"

"Did you finish watching? Did you see their joining?"

"No! And I won't. I won't watch any more."

"Please. I'll move it to the end. You'll see. Marissa wants Kytar."

"Just leave me alone," Shelley screamed. "I feel sick. I need to be alone."

Frowning, Pella hesitated a moment before backing out of the bedroom and closing the door.

Shelley fought to regain her control. She had to find Marissa and rescue her. First though she had to escape Talcor's clutches. She had to get out of here before he moved forward with his threat to collar her. Somehow she knew, once she wore his collar, she'd never leave Darinth. How could he have helped subjugate Marissa? She hadn't thought he was so cruel but apparently she'd been wrong. She had to escape.

Shelley washed her face and rinsed her mouth. She'd hoped Jared would help her but his loyalty was clearly with

Pella. Amazing what a good fuck would do to a man. Shelley shook her head, she couldn't worry about Jared. He obviously wasn't worried about her.

It still stung that he'd chosen a milk toast over her. She ignored the fact Talcor had chosen differently. She refused to see any good in the other woman. She was too afraid for Marissa.

The house was quiet. Now was her chance to escape, before Talcor returned. Quickly changing her robe, the only thing she had to wear, she briefly wondered what had happened to her clothes.

Creeping slowly downstairs, Shelley could hear Pella and Jared talking in the dining room. Good, the doorway was back from the stairs. If she could only get to the bottom without being seen, she could escape.

Chapter Thirteen

ഇ

Talcor raced his air car, anger and frustration making his driving a little erratic, a little careless. He didn't know how much longer he would be able to contain himself. Yet he knew he had to. Shelley just wasn't ready. She was moving closer to acceptance and he only hoped she'd surrender soon before his patience wore thin. He gunned the air car, narrowly avoiding two others as he landed at Davo's. Shoving aside the problem of Shelley, he forced his attention back to the reason for this visit.

He still had trouble accepting that an off-world male could feel the binding but he couldn't deny Jared and Pella felt linked, though they hadn't even started the process. It felt good to dump the problem in Davo's lap, especially since it was Davo's fault that Talcor faced the necessity of dealing with Shelley.

Davo ushered Talcor into the study. "Would you like a drink? I'm sure Shelley has driven you to that point by now."

"Close but not quite, and it's a little early for me," Talcor answered.

"Really?" Davo shot an intense look at Talcor. "I thought maybe you're visiting me to rant about Shelley."

"I'm quite capable of taking care of Shelley. She's not the problem this morning."

"Then what is the problem that causes such an early morning visit?"

"You know Shelley brought a man with her?"

Davo nodded. "The whole planet knows he tried to interfere and you showed him mercy."

Talcor shrugged. "He was ignorant and is no threat. Indeed, quite the opposite. He's been touched by the magic and he wants to bond with Pella."

Davo stared at Talcor, and said, "He *what*? Pella's been your companion for years. Before Shelley arrived, everyone thought you two would eventually take the final step. How do you feel about it?"

Talcor shrugged. "Part of me will miss Pella but we've always known it would end one day. Unlike everyone else, we knew the bond couldn't go further. I've felt the link between Pella and Jared despite the fact that he doesn't know the words. They need to bond. It will not be denied."

"But he's an off-worlder!"

"So are Marissa and Shelley," Talcor replied smoothly. "If females can be bound by our magic, why not males?"

"An off-world male? One not trained in our ways? Feeling the bonding urge? How can that be?"

"I would not presume to explain Darinthian magic. I'm here because Pella has asked that I instruct him in our ways."

"You haven't, have you?"

"Just enough to know they are serious. I believe they feel the magic."

"One of our sacred rules has been not to tell off-worlders."

"We made that rule when we thought there was no possibility of them understanding or feeling the bonds."

Davo nodded. "True. We never thought female off-worlders could feel the magic but given Marissa's and Shelley's responses we know they can."

"Still, a male that is spineless? Isn't that a mockery of our beliefs?"

"Spineless in your opinion. Obviously Pella doesn't feel the same. Is that the problem? Even though you knew you wouldn't finish the binding you feel rejected by her choice?"

"It is a hard thing to accept. She always seemed to enjoy my touch. How can she bind with a man who will not dominate her? Did she never enjoy what we had?"

"Or is it that she enjoys many different kinds of sex?"

Talcor shrugged. "Perhaps. Regardless of the reason, I need to know if I may initiate Jared and explain what is needed for the binding."

Talcor watched silently as Davo paced the room, his brow furrowed and his fists clenched. Finally, he stopped. Turning to Talcor, he said, "You have my permission. I will inform the rest of the elders of this development. Perhaps this is a way out of our current difficulties."

"Yes, that was in my mind as well. Another supply of men and women from off-world might alleviate the lack of bonded pairs. Maybe the magic just requires a new influx of possibilities. I will keep you advised on this development."

"As well as your own progress?"

Talcor sighed. "Of course."

Talcor left, a little troubled by the changes that might soon occur because of Pella's and Jared's binding. It would rock Darinth. A small part of Talcor had thought Davo would refuse. Off-worlders binding under Darinthian law foreshadowed many changes. As word of Darinthian customs spread, the fear and distaste of the rest of the galaxy might fade. Subsequently, the planet might be inundated by those seeking a magic that was rare and unlikely to happen for many. Even Darinthians struggled to find their mate. How much more difficult the task if the energies were confounded by outsiders. Or was it that the energy needed new blood? Talcor had been seeking his mate for a decade with no success until he met Shelley. Was it possible that many other mates lived off-world? What would an influx of off-worlders do to their close-knit society?

Talcor sighed. Luckily this was an issue for the elders. He didn't have to solve the problem. He did however have one more thing to do before he returned to his continuing battle with Shelley.

He hadn't checked with Kytar recently. Kytar should know of the latest developments.

Talcor looked up at his ancestral home. The high turrets rising from the mountainside shouted a stability and strength that he wasn't sure he felt right now. If Kytar and Marissa weren't there, he would have brought Shelley here where she'd have no possibility of escape or rescue, where they could focus on each other without interruption. Alas, when he'd agreed to let Marissa and Kytar are use the place he hadn't known he might want it. Years had passed since the last time he'd locked himself up in the mountain fortress. Alone, it wasn't attractive. It was a cold, stone monstrosity. Even Pella's company hadn't been enough to fill the place. A startling thought of Shelley pregnant with his child flitted across his mind. Shelley and children could fill the empty space. Suddenly he was eager to bring her here.

As Talcor stood staring at his ancestral home, Kytar opened the front door and waved Talcor closer.

Kytar gripped Talcor's forearm in greeting. "What news?"

"Why would you think there'd be news?" Talcor grinned, realizing just how much he'd missed his friend.

"You wouldn't be visiting us otherwise."

Talcor nodded. "Marissa's friend Shelley is on Darinth."

"Is she protected?"

"Yes," Talcor answered.

"You don't sound very happy about it."

"Were you happy to bind with an off-worlder?"

Kytar eyed Talcor. His face lost its smile. "Not at first, but now, oh yes. Marissa is well worth the trouble she caused me." Kytar shrugged. "The ritual was worth it."

"Shelley will never get a chance to ask for it," Talcor replied, his voice flat and determined. "She's already accepted my collar and Davo has strict instructions not to interfere. There'll be no challenge ritual."

"You feel the binding magic that strongly?" Kytar asked, his voice rising in an attempt to control his laughter. But he couldn't control his smile.

"Shelley is mine."

"Shelley! Why are you talking about Shelley?" Marissa swept through the doorway, her companion robe flowing. Hair unbound and a gleaming collar around her throat, she looked like a fairy princess, taking Talcor's breath away.

He bowed. "You look much happier than the last time I saw you."

Marissa's laugh tinkled over the men. "Oh yes, I am quite happy and quite satisfied," she said as her eyes locked with Kytar's. Then she shook herself. "But what about Shelley? Why are you talking about her?"

"She's here."

"Here? Where?" She asked looking around.

"Not here. At my house in the city."

"Shelley's here! I want to see her!"

"No," Kytar said, smiling, eyes gleaming. "We're not finished here." He paused. "And Talcor is not finished with your friend."

Marissa's breath hitched. "What do you mean?"

"Shelley and I have completed the first stage. She's agreed to accept my collar."

Talcor had shown Marissa hidden depths, and stunned, she had realized that he was the type of man she could imagine with Shelley. "But you haven't collared her yet? Why?"

"I don't think she's ready."

"But she's Shelley — she'll never be ready. You just need to finish the ritual."

"Will she stop fighting then?"

"Oh no, but then you really don't want her to, do you?"

Talcor frowned at Marissa. "I don't understand."

Marissa laughed. "No, you wouldn't. How do I explain?" she mussed as she walked up to Kytar and stroked his face.

"For as long as I've known her, Shelley has always challenged the men in her life. She fought for control of the relationship until she had it then she'd move on to the next man. Shelley has always sought a man strong enough to control her or at least an equal partnership. Shelley's tired of always being the one in control. I know she longs to find a strong man. By waiting to collar her, even if it is in her best interest, you appear weak and Shelley will drive a wedge into that weakness if you let her. Yes, she'll still fight after you bond. The fighting will be different though. It will be a battle of wills I think you'll both enjoy."

"You advocate against your friend? You tell me her secrets?"

"Talcor, if I didn't know the man you are, I wouldn't help you." Marissa cocked her head. "But I can see you and Shelley together and clearly the magic of the binding agrees."

Talcor eyed Marissa, processing her words. She made sense. Most of his women were like Pella—willing and compliant, the perfect submissive. He hadn't realized that an independent woman could possibly please him. Please him beyond imagining. He loved the way Shelley fought then submitted with her entire being. Her struggles and willfulness were intoxicating to the point that his control fled. If he didn't finish the binding soon, he might not be able to last. It was time for Shelley to learn her place. Nodding, Talcor left the mansion, eager to finish the binding.

* * * * *

Shelley wasn't sure where she was going but she couldn't stay in this place a moment longer. Terrified by her response to

Talcor, she knew she had to get away from him before she surrendered her will to him. Besides, much as she hated to admit it, with Talcor gone the house seemed empty and cold. Pella had told her to wait for an explanation and she'd begged Shelley to continue watching the vid until the end then she'd see how gracefully Marissa had submitted to Kytar.

Shelley didn't want to see that. She didn't know how Marissa had been brainwashed but that wasn't her friend she saw on the vid. That woman was a stranger to Shelley.

The front door was unlocked and Shelley hesitated. Would an alarm go off? She didn't see any blinking lights and she'd never seen Pella or Talcor lock the door. Maybe there was no crime on Darinth, she thought with a bitter laugh as she gently pulled open the door and walked into the street.

Taking a moment to get her bearings, Shelley decided she should go toward the arrival center. Surely there were hotels in that area. Her footsteps echoed in the quiet street. The afternoon had turned cloudy and dark. It seemed to close around her. She could barely see the next street in the growing darkness. Shelley shivered. She needed to find a hotel before the storm broke.

Nervous about being alone on a strange planet, she imagined someone was following her. Were those footsteps behind her? She turned to look but saw nothing. When she turned to continue walking, she ran into a hard male chest.

A startled squeak escaped. Where the hell had he come from? Heart racing, she moved to step around him.

"Not so fast," he said, reaching out and grabbing her arm.

Shelley tried to jerk away but his grip tightened until she was sure she'd be bruised.

"You're an off-worlder. What are you doing out alone?"

"Let go of me," demanded Shelley.

With a quick flick of his hand, Shelley found herself on her knees. "Answer my question. What are you doing out alone?"

"I don't have to tell you anything," she retorted.

The man stilled, frowning down at her.

Shelley tried to stand but he easily prevented her from regaining her feet.

Finally he said, "You wear a companion robe but no collar. You're linked. Who is your protector and where is he? You shouldn't be in this area alone. It isn't safe."

"So stop assaulting me and let me —"

"Don't speak to me with your senseless demands. Behave as a companion should," he interrupted, "or I'll treat you like the slut you are acting."

The man's cold, uncompromising tone frightened Shelley. She looked up to see his eyes boldly roaming her body. He lingered a moment on her breasts, much as the men in the arrival center had done.

"Answer me! Who is your protector?"

"I've escaped him and I don't need a protector," said Shelley with a defiant toss of her head that was spoiled by the sudden empty feeling deep inside and the weakness in her stomach. Indeed, if she hadn't already been on the ground, she probably would have ended up there anyway. Who was this man? And what business was it of his? Her anger flared but before it could explode, the man spoke again.

"You deny your link?" The man asked in a slow, soft voice.

* * * * *

Talcor entered his home and knew immediately that Shelley wasn't inside. Where was she? "Pella!"

Pella came scurrying from the dining room. "Yes, Master?"

"Where is Shelley?"

"In her bedroom," Pella hesitated. "She wasn't feeling well."

153

"She's not there!"

"Talcor?"

"Go look if you don't believe me!"

Pella threw him a scared look and raced upstairs. Jared stood in the dining room doorway. Concern lined his face.

"What happened?" Talcor asked in a menacing tone as he moved toward Jared.

He shrugged. "She was being Shelley."

"Explain."

"She was upset about the vid."

"What vid?"

Jared, not realizing his mistake, said, "She watched part of a vid about Marissa —"

"She what? It was the challenge ritual, wasn't it? How did she even know about it?" he roared at Pella who was halfway down the stairs.

"Talcor...Master, I'm so sorry. She just kept pushing. I didn't know how to say no," Pella stammered out in a rush. "She was so insistent and demanding but then she wouldn't watch it all. She stopped it after the first stage."

"And then you and Jared just let her go? You know she's not safe!"

"She was in the bedroom. She was sick. She said she needed to rest and ordered me out."

"She's not in the bedroom now, is she?"

Pella, her eyes glistening, sadly shook her head.

Talcor struggled with his anger. Pella and Jared had placed Shelley in unimaginable danger. Even now he could feel her anxiety. She was scared about something. It wasn't their fault. He should have collared her and bound her. His hesitation had created this problem.

Before he could say more, Talcor doubled over. A crack, a tear in his heart and he knew without a doubt that Shelley had repudiated their link in a public venue. This was so much more than the crack caused by Pella's repudiation.

Despite the severity of the betrayal, the link wasn't dead yet. It would take his agreement to finalize the break and that was something he would never do. Shelley wouldn't so easily gain her freedom, especially since she was in danger. He could feel the threat to her. He had to reach her before she was irrevocably lost.

"You two stay here. I'm going to find her," he said as he hurried through the doorway.

* * * * *

Shelley hesitated, remembering her conversation with Pella about the dangers of being without the protection of a man. Yet she couldn't admit Talcor's hold on her. "I'm not any man's slave," she stated, pushing aside her fear. "Now let go of me!"

The stranger's grip tightened, keeping her on her knees.

"Let me go!" Shelley screamed again.

The stranger laughed at Shelley's demand. "You foolish woman, you just denied your status as a protected companion. As an off-worlder you had no rights other than what a Darinthian man would grant you. No Darinthian will tolerate such disrespect," he said, dragging her to her feet. "You don't deserve the honor of wearing this," he stated, and with one quick motion he stripped off her companion robe, leaving Shelley wearing only sandals.

Shelley cursed herself for her stupidity in thinking that she could find Marissa or do anything alone on this planet. Where was Talcor when she needed him? She'd thought Talcor was scary but this man was terrifying.

"Let me show you the error of denigrating our customs," the man said as he dragged her down the street. "I think you'll enjoy a stay in our pleasure dome. Or rather, the men who patronize it will enjoy your silly defiance. You might not enjoy the consequences of their needs."

The man forced Shelley toward a large domed building. She gulped as she recognized the building. She remembered what Jared had told her he'd heard about this dome. She swallowed hard. It couldn't be that bad, could it?

Surely, the galactic council wouldn't condone such a place. She tried to pull away from the man. He just laughed and gripped her wrist harder until Shelley thought the bones might break. Frantically she looked around, trying to find someone to help her but the streets were deserted.

She screamed, "Talcor said I was under his protection. Let me go!"

"Talcor? Foolish woman. You denied your link with him. You've rejected his protection. He would have protected you. Any Darinthian male would have protected you, even me, but you've repudiated your link. You're an off-worlder who insults our customs. That simply isn't tolerable. You repudiated your protector in public. Do you think his ego will tolerate such an insult? Do you think I'll just let you go free?"

Shelley was temporarily blinded as the man dragged her into the darkness at the dome entryway. The darkness didn't seem to bother him. He didn't even slow down as he strode toward a door on the right. Still holding her tightly, pulling her along until he reached it. His grip didn't lessen as he pounded on the door.

Still trying to get her eyes to adjust to the low light level, Shelley was unprepared for the bright light coming from the room as the door opened. It took a few seconds before she realized a very elderly man stood in the doorway staring at her.

Finally he released her eyes and turned to the man holding her. "Soreng, what do you think you are doing? This woman doesn't belong here. She is bound. Even in your ignorance you should have felt the binding."

The man shrugged. "Gatekeeper, I found her wandering alone outside. She says she's not bound. She's damaged the link. Besides, she's an off-worlder. She doesn't deserve to be bound. She doesn't deserve our protection."

The old man turned his gaze back to Shelley and stared intently, as if he could see into her soul, making her squirm and wish there were some way to cover her nakedness.

"Her bond is still there. Faint but there." He shook his head. "This is not good," he muttered to himself. "Girl, do you repudiate your bond?"

"I'm not a girl. I'm a woman."

"Then act like one and answer me. Do you repudiate your bond?"

Shelley's captor said, "It doesn't matter if the link is entirely broken. It soon will be. Can you imagine any Darinthian man accepting such an insult?"

"Do not interrupt," the elderly man roared. "You have pushed our customs to the edge Soreng. Do not break them. She is a companion. You are pledged to protect her, not bring her here," the gatekeeper warned.

Shelley's captor seemed to wilt a little under the warning. She'd thought him big and scary but the gatekeeper person seemed to easily control him. *What is it with this planet*, wondered Shelley. Power seemed to be connected to sex and ritual and the gatekeeper's reminder about it caused the man to lose face.

"I haven't broken our customs! She has! She denied her protector! Take her! Put her to use," Shelley's captor demanded.

The gatekeeper fixed his eyes on Soreng. "Yes, I will take her and treat her with the respect due a companion. Perhaps if you followed custom a little better you would not still be single. You forget your place. She's not yet free."

"Who ever bound this woman didn't value her or cherish her. He let her wander into this section alone and unprotected.

I've struggled to find even one companion while her protector has been lax with his. He doesn't deserve this one. Take her or I'll bind her and make her life hell and you know I can."

"Perhaps that is why you have not found a companion, Soreng. You twist our customs and ignore them at your will. The magic recognizes your deficiencies." The gatekeeper glared at the man. Once Soreng seemed sufficiently wilted, the gatekeeper turned his eyes to Shelley, and said, "So be it. I will safeguard you until your protector arrives. By then you might be better equipped to make a rational decision."

"That's not what I want! I want you to use her in the dome."

"You know I will not do that unless her companion repudiates the link. Leave us now before he arrives and kills you for your interference."

The man shoved Shelley toward the gatekeeper. She would have lost her balance without his help. He was old and looked weak but when Shelley tried to pull away, his grip around her arm proved unbreakable.

"First, I think you need a tour of the facility. Perhaps then you will appreciate the protection you've been offered by a Darinthian man. Perhaps you just need a reminder that life is not always kind and women are not always treated with respect on Darinth," the gatekeeper said as he forced Shelley deeper inside the dome.

"Could I have some clothes?"

"No. Nakedness is normal on Darinth. Get used to it," he replied as he led Shelley into a dark tunnel. He paused and suddenly a part of the wall slid back. Behind the glass was a well-lit room. A woman was chained to the wall, her breasts crisscrossed with whip lines. Her head sagged and she looked defeated.

"No woman can long withstand the punishment meted out here," the gatekeeper stated. "Look at her. She has only been here two days. She will not last another one."

Shelley's stomach roiled. "How can you allow this to happen?"

"This has long been our custom. We cater to those prurient interests, those who know nothing of our customs. This is the Darinth the galaxy expects. We merely give them what they want. That woman chose to come here, despite the warnings. You will not find any Darinthian females here. They know better. The traumatized and misguided find their way here."

"Can she leave if she finds it's not what she expected?"

The man gave her a sad smile. Reaching out, he flicked a switch, and said, "Dorothea, do you wish to stop? Do you wish to leave Darinth?"

The woman raised her head, a panicked look on her face. "No, Master! Please don't send me away!"

The old man looked at Shelley and shrugged. "It is her choice."

"But that's not right," Shelley protested.

The gatekeeper shrugged.

On a sigh, Shelley asked, "What will happen to her?"

"What do you think?"

"You kill her or let her be killed?"

"You do not have a high opinion of us, do you?" The gatekeeper sounded amused. "No, she will be given medical attention and eventually sent back to her world. She will not die, though she might wish she had. Readjustment is sometimes very painful."

"Why can't you let her go now? Before she's hurt any more?"

"Because she asked for this and we honor off-worlder wishes."

"Really? Then this off-worlder wants to leave," said Shelley.

The gatekeeper chuckled. "You are a bound companion. Even if I let you go, the magic would not. Stop!" he ordered as Shelley started a rebuttal. "You know nothing of our customs. Are you so unwilling to learn more about what it means to be the valued companion of a Darinthian male? Are you so ignorant you refuse information that might contradict your stubborn beliefs?"

Shelley hesitated, looking at the woman beyond the glass. Talcor hadn't beaten her that way. He hadn't been cruel, just dominant. It seemed as though the men on this planet had created a continuum of domination that ranged from light control to devastating cruelty. But how did she know that Talcor might not swing to the far extreme. Could she really stay with him and trust him not to go too far?

As if reading her mind, the gatekeeper said, "No Darinthian man permanently damages his companion either mentally or physically. They cannot. The magic will not let them."

"What about Soreng?"

"Soreng is a perfect example. No Darinthian woman will bind with him. They simply do not feel the magic. The whole point of our system is to provide our females with protection and he is punished for not doing so. Come along, there's more to see. I want you to be very clear on the difference between companionship and the slavery you claim our companionship is. You need to experience a little more of what happens here," said the gatekeeper while closing the window. He led Shelley deeper into the dark tunnel.

* * * * *

Talcor left the house. He knew Shelley's general direction and the fact of her probable location caused him to clench his fists. He tried to avoid other men on the street but one came up to him and stood in his way.

"I found your property, Talcor," Soreng mocked. "I took her to the dome. That's the only acceptable place for off-world women.

"You are pledged to protect any companion."

"Oh, I made sure she renounced you first. I haven't broken any rules."

"But you've bent them beyond recognition. Do you really think I'll let you get away with such a traitorous act?"

"No, it is you who denigrate our customs by offering protection to an off-worlder. They don't deserve our respect and protection!"

"You deny the linking magic? You dare to question what I felt?" Talcor asked, his voice deceptively soft.

"Yes!"

Talcor shook his head. "Your repudiation of Darinthian customs has been noted. I'll let the council deal with you. In the meantime, Shelley is mine. I will not repudiate her and I will have her back."

"She was wandering alone. She denied her bonding with you. All you have to do is finalize the repudiation. You don't really want to bond with an off-worlder, do you? Repudiate her!" screamed Soreng as Talcor turned and strode toward the dome.

"That's not going to happen," Talcor muttered to himself, hoping it wasn't already too late. He could feel Shelley's fear, and her emotional turmoil fed his anxiety. He needed to reach her before she was lost to him forever. Talcor strode toward the dome. He'd been inside just once before. He fought to quell his rising gorge at the thought of her in the dome. At least she couldn't be a prisoner yet. They were still linked. He hadn't renounced the link. She had to be safe.

Chapter Fourteen

ℛ

Shelley found herself stumbling along with the gatekeeper. They went deeper and deeper into the dark tunnel before he stopped and opened another window. Moving in front of her, he blocked her vision of the room, and said, "This may be very disturbing for you. Know that it is the woman's wish, not ours." Then he moved aside.

The room was dim, lit only by a single torch on the far wall. Shelley's eyes adjusted as she searched the room and found a small woman, fully dressed, sitting at a small table. The rest of the room was empty. The woman looked bored and anxious at the same time. She sipped a drink, her eyes constantly scanning the room. She clearly couldn't see out the window where Shelley watched.

After a few moments, part of the wall slid aside and a man entered. Shelley knew immediately that he wasn't Darinthian. The man was big but not quite big enough, not quite masculine enough.

As if in response to her thought, the gatekeeper said, "He's an off-worlder who wants to sample Darinthian sex."

"But if he's an off-worlder, how do you keep the woman safe?"

"This woman refused safety," the gatekeeper responded.

"She what?"

"Many off-world women ask for things without realizing the consequences of their requests."

"But you can't let her do this!"

"I said this would be hard for you," he replied. "Watch."

Back in the room, the man took two steps then gestured for the woman to come closer. She slowly stood and moved near him.

Shelley gasped as he suddenly reached out and tore off the woman's blouse. Her breasts overflowed her lacy bra, her nipples clearly outlined by the thin material.

"Strip!" the man ordered.

The woman smiled and reached behind her back, flicking the clasp of her bra. As the garment fell to the floor, the woman cupped her breasts and lifted them toward the man. A fleshy offering he rejected by backhanding the woman's face. Her head snapped back and she fell to her knees.

"Do as I tell you. Nothing more," the man said. "Now stand and finish stripping."

The woman shook her head and fought her way to her feet.

Shelley could see a vivid read splotch where she'd been hit. Shelley bit back an exclamation of anger, telling herself that the woman had asked to be treated this way. Though Shelley couldn't understand why anyone would want to be degraded like that.

The woman removed her shoes and her skirt. Head down, she stood naked in front of the man. He smiled and circled her. His eyes were intense, inventorying the woman's assets before reaching into his pocket and pulling out vicious-looking nipple clamps.

Shelley's cunt clenched at the sight of the sharp teeth on the clamps. These weren't simple erotic devices, they were instruments of torture and the poor woman didn't even know they were coming since the man stood at her back and reached around her.

He lightly stroked her breasts before grasping a nipple and quickly snapping a clamp on. The woman screamed and tried to move away as he gave her other breast the same treatment. The woman went to her knees, her face contorted in pain.

The man, showing no mercy, grabbed her arm and dragged the woman to a wall. He touched something and the wall slid back, revealing chains. He forced the woman's arms wide and clamped each wrist. Then kneeling before her, he grabbed an ankle and forced the woman's legs wide. More clamps appeared. Forcing both ankles far apart he fastened the restraints. From a shelf, he took an evil-looking device.

It slowly dawned on Shelley that the device was a dildo. She hadn't recognized it because of its strange shape. It had two prongs. The prongs started small and widened into huge bases. The size alone wasn't too bad but the prongs weren't smooth. About halfway down toward the widest part, the prongs were covered in points that looked sharp and painful. She gasped. No woman could take something like that. She'd be ripped apart.

"Stop him," Shelley moaned, her cunt clenched in sympathy for what was about to assault the woman. Moving to step away from the scene before her, she backed into the gatekeeper. She hadn't realized the gatekeeper stood so close behind her.

He pressed forward, forcing her against the glass. "You will watch and learn the difference between companionship and that travesty."

Shelley shook her head, "No..."

"Yes."

The man knelt in front of the woman. He inserted the tips of the dildo. The woman squirmed and Shelley saw moisture leaking down her leg. The man wiggled the dildo, gradually sliding it in about an inch. Shelley watched the woman smile and wiggle some more. She obviously had no idea what was coming. The man looked up and grinned before using all of his strength to shove the dildo home. The woman screamed before sagging against the chains.

Shelley saw blood trickling down the woman's stomach — from the nipple clamps she realized — before it mixed with the blood trailing down the woman's thighs.

"Stop it! Stop it!" Shelley cried, tears streaming down her face.

"Do you now see the difference?"

No sex, just violence. No love, just a woman as object. Shelley swallowed hard, graphically seeing the difference in what Talcor offered versus what she'd thought of their customs. She shuddered. She didn't want to be stuck in this hellhole. How could she escape? Would Talcor come for her? Or would he consider himself well rid of her? Why had she been foolish enough to reject him?

Talcor's strength, his control, gave her the freedom to be herself. She could fight and not worry that she'd defeat him because that wasn't going to happen.

"I understand," Shelley whispered.

"You publicly renounced your link to your protector, foolish woman. You left yourself unprotected on this planet. A very dangerous action, don't you think?"

"Yes..." Shelley trailed off, genuinely frightened by this old man who seemed like the hardest man she'd ever met.

"You're a very lucky woman," the gatekeeper said as he cocked his head as if listening. "Your protector has not renounced you. He is here for you. Come."

The gatekeeper took her arm. Shelley felt too shocked to protest or move without help as he led her back to the entryway.

* * * * *

Talcor entered the dome. He saw the gatekeeper leading Shelley toward him, her face white, eyes wide with fear.

"What have you done, Gatekeeper?" Talcor whispered.

The gatekeeper held up a hand. "I have merely shown your companion her choices."

"Have you broken her?"

The gatekeeper shook his head. "Merely frightened her."

Shelley roused from her stupor and wrenched away from the gatekeeper. Running to Talcor, she placed a hand on his chest. "Talcor...Talcor you...you have to help that woman."

Talcor's face hardened. His eyes blazing, he met the gatekeeper's implacable stare.

"That poor woman. She's being torn apart...bleeding..." Shelley's voice trailed off, and tears steamed down her face.

Talcor gathered Shelley close. He bent his head and murmured comfortingly into her hair, waiting until her trembling subsided.

Shelley drew in a shuddering breath as Talcor's warmth penetrated her shock. She pulled back a little so she could see his face. "Please help that poor woman."

"The woman is not your concern," the gatekeeper said. "Right now you have a more pressing concern. Will you willingly leave with your protector or will you stay here?"

"Talcor —"

"I'm sorry, the gatekeeper is right. You've denied our bond. That must be rectified," he said, his voice hard, hiding his fear that Shelley might reject him again. If she did it in front of the gatekeeper, he'd have no choice but to leave her here, and from her obvious distress, he knew she wouldn't survive the experience. She might rail against him and cause him no end of grief but thankfully she wasn't broken yet and never would be if he had any say in the matter. He shoved aside his fear, and said, "Your choice. Say you accept me or stay here."

Shelley wanted to argue. She wanted to scream at him and the gatekeeper. How dare they ignore that woman's plight and force her to make a decision that wasn't really any choice at all?

Talcor frowned. As if hearing her thoughts, he said, "The woman whose fate concerns you made her choice. There is nothing I can do for her. Just as your fate is yours to decide. Come with me or stay here."

What choice did she have? She wouldn't stay in this place. Even as that thought moved in her mind, a thread of doubt crept in. If she was honest with herself, she didn't really want a choice. Did she?

She wanted to be with Talcor and seeing the travesty here in the dome just emphasized her decision. She wasn't fleeing the dome as much as running to Talcor. His actions were loving and gentle, even if sometimes painful. With a sigh of regret, she left the woman to her fate, and said, "I want to go with you."

Talcor felt a sudden tension in the magic as Shelley's public acceptance renewed their link. He knew they weren't through though. She'd defied him and terrified him. It was clearly long past time to finish the binding.

"You defied me by leaving my home. You repudiated our link. There is a price to pay for your defiance. You will be punished. Are you certain you wish to come with me and accept the hospitality of my house?"

Shelley swallowed hard. She'd never seen Talcor this hard. She glanced back at the gatekeeper, who stood patiently, as if awaiting her answer.

"Answer me. Do you accept my hospitality and protection?"

Shelley's anger flared but she fought it down. She wanted to defy him because she always fought but she knew she wasn't trapped. She knew she could say no. She also knew she didn't want to deny him ever again.

She recognized the implication of the question. Talcor wanted to assert his claim, to force her to admit their link. Accepting Talcor's hospitality would be forever this time. She defiantly tilted her head and looked into his ice-blue eyes. As if daring her to voice a protest, he remained silent.

Shelley knew she had no choice and that really she didn't want a choice. Whether she believed in the magic or not, she wanted Talcor's protection. "I accept your hospitality and protection," she whispered.

Talcor smiled. Hard hands held her head still as he said, "I claim you as mine. You are my companion. I own your body. I own your mind. I own your spirit. I claim you as mine."

This time Shelley recognized the snap of the link. Her stomach clenched and she fought to remain standing. Talcor pulled her close and entered her mind with the full force of his personality. "Breathe," he said as a cooling rush flushed through her. This time, she didn't fight his control. She surrendered herself to his domination and felt him move through her mind with a soothing touch that did nothing to lessen the sheer power of their bond.

Shivering from the intensity of the linking, Shelley realized she was still naked. No wonder she felt vulnerable and exposed. "Please, could I have some clothes?" she asked.

"No! You've lost the right to wear a companion's robe until you've fully paid your penance for your defiance. Be happy you still have sandals," Talcor said harshly. "Gatekeeper, do you have any rope?"

"Of course," he replied. He disappeared for a moment before returning with rope.

Shelley's heart nearly stopped as she realized the full extent of Talcor's determination. She swallowed hard, wanting to protest but knowing it was futile as Talcor grabbed her wrists and wrapped the rope around them before circling her neck, forcing her arms up between her breasts. He gave a little tug and the rope tightened around her throat. Not enough to choke her but definitely enough so she wouldn't forget it.

Shelley's cheeks flushed as she realized the gatekeeper stood smiling as he watched her degradation.

"Thank the gatekeeper for his kindness," Talcor ordered.

Shelley wanted to scream but she bit back her retort and said in a small voice, "Thank you, Gatekeeper."

"Oh you are most welcome. Talcor, I wish you good hunting," the gatekeeper said before disappearing into the darkness.

Shelley sighed with relief. "He's gone. You can let me go now."

Talcor laughed. "Oh we've barely started and the gatekeeper's presence had nothing to do with my treatment of you. Just wait until we get home."

Shelley gasped when Talcor tugged on the end of the rope, leading her like a dog into the street.

"No," she whispered. "You can't do this! I'm naked!"

"Yes you are, and now we demonstrate my control over you. I can do anything I wish. Keep up," Talcor ordered, walking fast toward his home.

Shelley stumbled behind him, suddenly terrified by his cruel treatment. Yes, she'd defied him, but so what? She didn't deserve this kind of treatment. She wanted to scream at him but was too afraid.

Talcor led Shelley along the street, headed toward his house. "I've had enough of your resistance. You have publicly humiliated me. This is a wrong you must set right. Your contrariness nearly caused you to become a slave in the pleasure dome. Would you really rather be a slave there than my honored companion? Are you so dense that you do not finally understand the difference?"

Shelley wanted to protest. He didn't have the right to force her to do anything. Yet she remained silent and tried to ignore the tendril of unease that Talcor's words aroused. The trip back to the house seemed far longer than her earlier journey.

Jared and Pella looked up as Talcor stormed into the study, dragging Shelley along behind him, her hands bound to her throat, the picture of submission.

"Pella, take Shelley to her bedroom, release the ropes and wait there with her. Jared, stay here."

Pella and Jared exchanged a glance before Pella moved to guide Shelley up the stairs.

Shelley's mind raced. She wanted to protest. She wanted to demand her freedom. Yet she longed for Talcor to take her and make her his companion for real. Heart racing, Shelley wondered if she'd destroyed everything by repudiating Talcor. He'd bound her again but wasn't that just to satisfy the gatekeeper? Why hadn't she listened to everyone who told her to just wait? Why did she always have to make her life so hard? Her eyes filled, though the tears didn't spill and she quickly blinked them clear,

Pella gave her a sideways glance and sighed. As they reached the bedroom door, Pella said, "Have you finally accepted your link with Talcor?"

Shelley shrugged, struggling with her tears, terrified of admitting her need.

"Talcor loves you. He was distraught when he found you'd gone. He'll accept you back and forgive you for your stupidity. He knows you're an off-worlder and our customs are strange to you," Pella said as she unbound Shelley's wrists.

Shelley stared at Pella. How could she have ever thought her vacuous? Just because Pella submitted didn't mean she was any less intelligent or less independent.

Swallowing her pride, Shelley whispered, "Help me."

Pella cocked her head. "Help you, what? What do you expect?"

Something deep inside Shelley seemed to break loose. Emotions flooded her and her tears escaped, spilling down her cheeks.

"What do you expect?" Pella asked softly.

"I know I've been stupid," Shelley admitted. "Your customs frighten me and I still don't really understand them."

"Yield to Talcor and he'll take care of you. Stop fighting him. That's all you have to do—stop fighting."

"If he's so great, why are you screwing around with Jared?" Shelley asked, trying to regain some of her pride.

"Jared and I are fated to be together, even as you and Talcor are fated."

"Aren't you jealous?"

Pella's laugh tinkled over Shelley like flowery bells. "Oh no, I am quite content with my place. As you should be with yours. Shelley, we're not in competition. The magic lets us each find what we need. Accept it."

Shelley turned her back on Pella and moved to the window. Shoulders shaking, she tried to suppress her sobs as she looked out the window and wondered what Talcor was doing with Jared and how much time she had before he came to take the final step in their linking.

* * * * *

Jared watched Talcor storm to the bar and take a quick drink, obviously struggling to control his anger. Jared remained silent, wondering if Shelley knew how much she'd infuriated Talcor. Jared wanted to run from Talcor's palpable anger but he didn't dare move.

Talcor closed his eyes and took a series of deep breaths. He was clearly trying to control his anger and Jared knew how he felt. Shelley could be quite trying. Jared was thankful Pella would be far more restful than Shelley.

Talcor opened his eyes and turned to Jared. "Be very, very glad your binding with Pella will not be fraught with such dissension and turmoil."

"Funny, I was just thinking the same thing," Jared replied.

Talcor stared at Jared for a moment before smiling and shaking his head. "I forgot you know what a trial Shelley can be."

Jared shrugged and smiled. "I'm not sorry Shelley is your responsibility now."

"Speaking of responsibilities... Davo has agreed that I may impart the knowledge you need to bind Pella. Since she's already been released from me, you only need the knowledge of the binding words."

"Shouldn't she be here?"

"What is done next is private between males." Talcor moved close to Jared. Reaching out he suddenly grabbed Jared by the throat. "Listen to me, off-worlder! If you hurt Pella, I will kill you. The ritual is dangerous and for once in your life you will need to be strong. If you aren't, both of you will die."

Jared glared at Talcor. "I might not be strong the way you are but I would never hurt Pella! Back off and teach me what I need to know."

Nodding, pleased with Jared's defiance, Talcor released Jared and took a step back.

"The claiming starts with the following words—I claim you as mine..." For the next hour Talcor explained the linking process, making Jared repeat the words and the ritual until Talcor was satisfied that Jared really could claim Pella and keep her safe.

"Off-worlder, you don't have a Darinthian collar, do you?"

Jared shook his head.

Talcor walked to his desk and pressed a button. A panel in the far wall opened. Talcor removed two collars from the safe. He closed the safe and moved toward Jared. He handed one of the collars to Jared. "I would be honored to supply Pella's collar."

"I am honored to accept your gift," Jared replied. He examined the device while Talcor pointed out its features.

Talcor concluded with one more warning. "You'll feel the link snap into place. You must control both your response and Pella's. If you don't, you'll both die."

Jared nodded. "I won't let any harm come to her. She is mine to protect."

"Then wait here and I'll send her to you," Talcor said while turning to leave.

Talcor hoped the two knew what they were doing but even he could see their strong connection, though they'd spoken no words at all. Tonight, Jared would claim Pella.

Talcor sighed. The final binding with Shelley would require all his energy. She couldn't remain free to get into any more trouble. It was time he made her his full companion, whether she was ready for it or not, he decided as he climbed the stairs to her bedroom.

Talcor silently opened the bedroom door and stood in the doorway. Pella leaned against the bedpost, motionless, just watching Shelley. Shelley didn't notice his appearance but Pella looked over at him. He gestured to her. Pella took one last glance at Shelley before stepping outside the room. Talcor reached behind her and softly closed the door.

Talcor cocked an eyebrow. "Are you sure about Jared?"

Tinkling laughter escaped. "How can you doubt?"

Meeting Pella's smile with one of his own, Talcor said, "Pella, you've been a valued companion. We've had many good times. I will miss you."

"No you won't, you'll have your hands full," she replied, nodding toward the bedroom.

"Probably," he said, reaching out to stroke her face. "Jared knows what he needs to do."

"The elders agreed?"

"Yes. What other choice did they have? Go to your companion."

"Thank you, Talcor!" Pella yelled as she raced down the stairs toward Jared.

Talcor grinned at her pleasure and exuberance before opening the door to Shelley's bedroom. He stood in the doorway, taking a moment to drink in Shelley's beauty. Her chin tilted and curly red hair tumbled down her straight back. Struggling to control his need, he focused his energies and took a deep breath, no trace of hesitation remained when he strode into the bedroom.

"It is time," Talcor said.

Shelley didn't move, only said, "Time for what?"

"You *know*."

Shelley remained silent.

"Shelley, it is time we finished our link. Accept my collar," he demanded.

A nearly overwhelming need to say yes roared through Shelley—a need she fought off. "No," she whispered.

Shelley ignored the pounding in her head. *There's no way I'll ever wear a man's collar...is there?* screamed through her mind, burying thoughts of acceptance. How could she have been so stupid? Davo had warned her. The ambassador had warned her. Talcor had warned her. Even Jared had expressed misgivings. She'd ignored them all. Now she was stuck in this room with a hard, unyielding Darinthian male fully confident of his own powers, apparently aided by magic or some kind of control over her.

"Shelley, it is time."

She glanced over her shoulder. "You're serious, aren't you? You really mean to do this?"

Talcor cocked an eyebrow and nodded. He held out his hand.

Shelley gulped, the lump in her throat nearly choking her. Talcor's eyes were cold and hard, his mouth a flat line. Shelley knew if she tried to refuse, he'd force her. The stern line of his body made it obvious that he'd brook no disobedience. She knew that his patience could no longer be tried. Nothing would protect Shelley from what was coming next. Lightheaded, she turned and placed her trembling hand in his.

He pulled her into his arms. Hands cupped her buttocks, pulling her so close that his hard chest flattened her breasts.

Shelley tried to inch back but Talcor easily held her. His warmth penetrated her, easing some of the chill she felt. She struggled to draw a breath but he seemed to take her very air. She stared at his chest, trying to calm her breathing, but he said, "Look at me."

She drew in a deep breath and tilted her chin, meeting his stare.

"Tell me you accept my collar."

"I already said that twice. Why do I have to say it again?"

"Your acceptance was negated when you repudiated our bond. It must be done again." Talcor placed a hand on Shelley's throat. "Your neck is bare without my collar. I will hear the words. Say you accept my collar."

Shelley felt Talcor's fingers flexing, nearly cutting off her air, causing a blinding wave of desire. Knees weak, she knew she'd met a man who could and would control her. A man whose strength would never let her down. A man who wouldn't flinch in the face of her raging demands.

Still she denied her need. She shook her head.

"I've had enough," Talcor roared. "By the laws of Darinth, we are bound and it is time you learned exactly what that means."

Shelley yanked free and backed up. Talcor followed her. He stalked forward—intent, dark and dangerous. His eyes cold with determination, Shelley knew pleas would go unheard. Her mind raged, wanting to scream a protest she knew would be futile. At the same time, her body weakened and melted at the strength of the man approaching.

How often had she longed for a man who wouldn't take no for an answer, a man who knew his own needs and yet a man willing to please her? Indeed, a man who could make her scream with need and longing, a man who could make her forget everything but the moment? A man who could turn off her mind?

Talcor continued his forward motion until Shelley was sandwiched between his hard chest and the cold window against her back. He threaded his fingers through her hair and tugged until her eyes met his. He bent and took her lips with his hard mouth while grinding his pelvis against her stomach. His rigid cock was huge and throbbing and she fleetingly realized that she wasn't the only one affected by the binding. Then all thoughts flew away.

Breaking off the kiss, Talcor said, "Foolish woman. There is no escape this time. You will kneel before me while I place my collar on your neck."

Moving his hands to her shoulders, he pushed her to her knees. He kept his grasp on her shoulders until she steadied.

Shelley shook so hard that even with his help it was difficult to stay upright. Part of her wanted to curl up on the floor at his feet and just hide. Before she could move though, Talcor gathered her hair and twisted it behind her shoulders, baring her throat.

She closed her eyes and shivered when he placed his large, hot hands on her bare neck. His thumbs caressed a line down her throat, pressing just a little. "Stop fighting me. Stop fighting the linking magic. Say you accept the collar, Shelley. You know I can and will convince you. You know you can't fight me and I'll wager a tiny part of you doesn't want to fight. Say the words, Shelley."

Shelley looked up the long line of his body into his hard, cold eyes and she clenched with need. Why was she still fighting what they both wanted? It was long past time to grow up and shove aside her fear and distrust. She swallowed, her neck moving against his hand before saying, "Talcor, I accept your collar."

A slow smile spread across his face and his eyes warmed as he stroked her neck once more.

Shelley stopped breathing as she felt the cold metal against her neck. She made a small motion but Talcor quickly circled her neck with the collar.

Talcor's words beat in her head. "I claim you as mine. You are my companion. I own your body. I own your mind. I own your spirit. I claim you as mine."

And as he said the last word, Shelley felt more than heard the click of the lock and the collar enclosed her neck, proclaiming her Talcor's property. She started to protest again but her protest turned to a scream as a blinding swell caused every muscle in her body to seize in a tight ball of agony. At the same time, a wave of heat and cold assaulted her. She felt Talcor's concern deep in her bones but she couldn't even scream anymore as she felt her entire body shake, totally out of her control.

Talcor abandoned any thought of a gentle binding as he felt Shelley's entire body spasm. He gathered her into his arms. He fought his own need, and said, "Breathe through the binding. Don't surrender to it. Stay in control," he told her as he felt his own control slipping away. He tightened his hold as she arched back, trying to escape the linking. He centered his thoughts, melding them with hers, trying desperately to find a spot that would lessen her agony so they could finish the binding. He ruthlessly entered her mind, demanding her obedience to his will.

Her thoughts were frantic. He couldn't feel any rationality. She'd turned into an animal—an animal in pain. He'd have to delve deeper. Kytar hadn't warned him that the binding would be this bad. Every Darinthian knew that linking was dangerous. If Talcor couldn't take control of the process he'd lose Shelley and that was just unacceptable. His resolve firmed. He tore a hole in her mental barrier and washed through her, ignoring her sobs, he forced her to submit to his will. Forcing her orgasm back from the brink.

"Damn you, let me come," Shelley finally whispered, her voice harsh with need.

"Not yet! Obey me!" Talcor continued his ruthless assault on her mind, calming her need until it passed and they were safe from death.

Shelley felt Talcor's voice as if from a great distance at the same time that it seemed to echo in her head. A blinding rush of release raced through her entire body as her orgasm receded, releasing all the tension that had built since Talcor said the binding words. Gasping for air, Shelley closed her eyes and surrendered to Talcor's hold. She trusted him to keep her safe.

Talcor stroked Shelley's hair. Still holding her, he looked down at her face. Lines of exhaustion creased her forehead. She wasn't unconscious, just too exhausted to do or say anything. He opened his senses and could feel her bruises, her ache. He'd seen vids of many linkings but he'd never seen a woman respond as Shelley had. Her response had nearly pushed him over the edge. It had been a close thing.

Kytar had told him he could influence Marissa's emotions after the collaring. As Talcor explored Shelley's emotions, he felt points he could nudge. A whisper of vulnerability where he could sway her. They'd made a strong bond and Talcor knew Shelley would have a tough time being angry now. He wouldn't let her anger consume her anymore.

Shelley's eyelids fluttered for a moment before her green eyes stared into his. "Why?" she sobbed. "Why did you stop my orgasm?"

"Because it would have meant both our deaths."

She didn't answer, didn't move, but Talcor could feel her exploring the bond, gently touching it. He sent warmth and concern down the link and her eyes opened wider.

"You're in my head," she whispered. "How can you be in my head?"

Talcor pushed down the panic in her mind. "You're safe."

"How can I be safe if you're in my head?" she asked, her voice gaining strength as she tried to be angry but she felt Talcor blocking it. "What did you do to me?"

"I collared you and claimed you. The ritual is magic. The magic not only accepted our bonding but made it strong and unbreakable."

"You make it sound as if magic is an entity apart from us."

Talcor shrugged. "Sometimes it seems that way. Every bonding is unique. We almost didn't make it."

"It hurt so much." Shelley tried to sit up but Talcor held her tightly.

"Rest a moment. Then we will consummate the binding."

"There's more? But this is terrible. I don't want any more. Let me go!" She pulled away.

"How can you still deny our binding?" Talcor stood and his mouth tightened. "How can you say it is terrible? We have a strong link. And now that we've completed the collaring, you are mine. I can do anything to you and you can't stop me. I'm bigger and stronger than you. The only protection you have is my good will and you are trying my temper. I've collared you. You've felt the binding but still you try to escape me? What kind of fool are you?" He turned away from her, shaking his head, he stared out the window and breathed deeply.

Shelley briefly felt his anger before he withdrew the warmth of his mind. She shivered. The room seemed to have grown noticeably colder. Had she pushed him too far?

Even as she wondered, Talcor turned back to her. "We are strongly linked. We will continue. The next step is consummation. I'll even let you have an orgasm," he said, striding back to her and grabbing her arms.

"You'll let me? You bastard! Let me go!" Shelley demanded, struggling to free herself from Talcor's grip.

"We've delayed this binding far too long. No more evasions Shelley. I am tired of your games. I was going to give you a brief rest but if you're strong enough to still fight, then you don't need it. We will finish this now," he said. Picking her up, he tossed her on the bed, keeping a firm grip on her wrists.

He pulled her arms over her head. Fastening one arm then the other. Grabbing an ankle, he chained it to the bedpost. Shelley tried to kick him with her free foot and nearly connected with his face before he captured her last unbound extremity and pulled her spread-eagle, to finish restraining her.

"We finish this now, Shelley," stated Talcor as he pulled off his shirt.

Chapter Fifteen

∞

Pella ran downstairs and flew into Jared's arms.

"Whoa," he said as she nearly knocked him off his feet.

She grinned up into his face. "Do it!"

"What? No anticipation, no delays, no qualms?"

Pella pulled back a little. "Not on my side. What about you?"

He pulled her close again, and said, "Pella, I claim you as mine. You are my companion. I own your body. I own your mind. I own your spirit. I claim you as mine."

Jared nearly lost control as the last words left his mouth and the binding snapped into place. He hadn't expected the linking to be so strong. He felt Pella move toward an orgasm. "No," he moaned as he grabbed her face and forced her eyes to his. "Hold tight. Breathe through the binding."

Pella's eyes slowly regained their focus. She shuddered as her energies dissipated and she regained her feet. "Keep going," she demanded.

"You're too weak to continue to the next stage."

"No, I'm not. I want this over as soon as possible."

"As do I, but Talcor has filled my head with cautions. The collaring will be worse that the first binding. You're shaking and weak. We'll wait at least a few minutes before continuing."

"No! Continue! Now! I've waited my whole life for such a link. I'll wait no longer."

"Pella, you'll wait until I say we continue," Jared said, his voice soft but firm as he pulled her to the sofa. Sitting, he pulled her onto his lap and kissed her deeply and thoroughly. His hand moved to her shirt, unbuttoning it and pushing it back from her shoulders. His fingers toyed with one nipple then the other.

"Jared, you can't play with me like this. Finish the binding so we can fully satisfy each other."

"Pella, you of all women should realize that at this moment, I'm in control."

Pella's eyes widened. Jared grinned at her. "That's right. I might not be as dominant as Talcor but I will control our linking. You will accept my timing, won't you?"

Pella smiled and nodded, surrendering herself to Jared's touch. She barely noticed as he stripped her naked. She lost track of time as she sank into the gentle sensations coursing through her until finally, Jared asked, "Pella, will you accept my collar?"

"Oh yes, I accept your collar."

Jared took a deep breath, gearing himself to complete the binding and make Pella his. His fingers lightly caressed her throat before reaching under her hair and threading the collar around her neck. "I claim you as mine. You are my companion. I own your body. I own your mind. I own your spirit. I claim you as mine."

Pella arched across Jared's lap. Unsure of his own power, he ruthlessly pushed himself into Pella's mind and forced her back from her orgasm. She moaned and he wondered how much longer this would take, how much longer he could hold on, when he felt a blissful cold wave bounce between them and suddenly Pella was back. He'd done it! He'd made Pella his! They were bound now. He looked down into her sweaty face and realized just how much the binding had taken from her. He placed a gentle kiss on her lips before standing and carrying her to his bedroom where he placed Pella on the bed.

Opening her arms and reaching up to him, Pella said, "Let's finish our binding."

Climbing on top of her, Jared opened his pants and gathered her close. With a firm stroke, he buried his cock deep into her cunt.

* * * * *

Exposed and helpless, Shelley watched Talcor strip off his clothes. Muscles bulged as he bent to remove his shoes and pants. Then he stood fully erect and waited.

The sight of him naked nearly stopped her heart. He was muscular without being muscle-bound. Wide shoulders narrowed to a tight waist and powerful thighs. Seated between his legs, his fully erect cock jutted toward her. She knew he was large but to see him in his full glory was a little frightening and very arousing. She itched to touch him, to follow each muscle from start to finish, to fondle his balls and test their weight in her hands. His skin gleamed as if oiled, his very stance proclaiming his power. She wanted to feel that power. She wanted him to press her into the bed. She wanted him deep inside. She wanted him and she cursed herself for her foolish denial of that fact.

Jerking her eyes away from Talcor's cock, she met his gaze. He smiled and Shelley's breath hitched. Her cunt dripping moisture, she admitted she'd never wanted a man the way she wanted Talcor. Why did she still fight him? How silly to fight when all she wanted was his huge cock ramming into her pussy.

She felt tendrils moving in her head as Talcor sifted through her emotions. Emotions she couldn't hide or deny any longer. "You're beginning to understand Darinthian magic, aren't you?"

Shelley nodded.

"But you still have doubts."

Shelley nodded again.

Talcor cocked his head, his blue eyes as intense as lasers. "I would be soft with you but that is not what you want, is it? I can feel your need, your desire for a strong man. You can't hide from me, Shelley. Let me give you what you want. Beg for release. Beg me to satisfy you."

Shelley's eyes widened as Talcor moved to sit on the edge of the bed. His cock nearly in her face, the memory of licking and sucking that cock rushed back.

Talcor reached over and stroked her cheek. "I'll make it easy for you. We'll play a game. I like games. You fight as much as you like. You deny me all you want and I'll ignore your protests. Not only will I ignore them, I'll subvert them until you are begging for release from the sensations I'll generate. I'm in your head now, Shelley. I know what you want."

Talcor leaned down and captured Shelley's lips. His kiss feathered across her lips before trailing down her neck. She felt his energies a moment before his hands circled her waist. He massaged her abdomen before moving to her pelvis. His hand covered her from side to side. *Am I that small or is he just that big?* she wondered before his hands moved to her thighs and stroked them. Shelley could feel moistness seeping from her cunt. She longed to beg him to touch her clit, to insert at least a finger into her cunt—to give her something.

Shelley squirmed and pulled at her restraints. Talcor ignored her motions and continued his gentle caresses. Shelley shivered as Talcor massaged her foot. She had no protection on this world. So used to the men of her world, men who accepted the word no, men who'd never dream of simply claiming a woman. Talcor had no such restraints. Here on Darinth, in his own home, he was king and she was dependent upon his kindness. She wanted to scream at the injustice of it. She didn't belong to any man.

Yet I don't want to leave him. She didn't know where the thought had come from but she knew the truth of it. She'd felt more alive in the last few days than ever in her life. She wanted Talcor's hands on her body and his mouth on hers. She was tired of her denials. She longed to belong to him. It felt right even if it made no sense.

Talcor worked his way back up her body, stroking her legs before burying his tongue in her pussy. Shelley moaned as he licked and suckled her clit. His fingers played at her entrance, teasing but not entering.

Shelley tilted her chin, looking down at Talcor's bent head. The sight of him nestled between her legs sent another arch of need throughout her body. "I surrender," she said before she thought about the words or their meaning.

Talcor's head jerked up. He cocked an eyebrow, obviously surprised by her words. She felt him in her head. She felt his happiness when he realized her surrender was real. Surrender with enough resistance to make it fun. He crawled up her body. Reaching out, he grabbed her hair. Looming over her, he forced her head back. Holding her there for a moment, his eyes on hers, he smiled down, and said, "I accept your surrender. Let's play."

Shelley's nipples tightened more, reaching toward him. He lightly brushed a hand across them. "Lovely," he murmured, bending his head to bestow a quick lick on each nipple. Shelley's pelvis clenched, wanting more stimulation than a quick lick. But she stayed quiet.

Talcor's mind touched hers. She felt more than heard his whisper deep in her head. *You're mine.*

She gasped when he stroked a pleasure center in her mind. He moved to hold her head in his hands. Eyes locked with hers, he moved deep in her head and briefly touched a pain center. He moved back and forth.

We're linked on a level I had not expected, he thought.

"You can't do this!" Shelley cried.

Talcor smiled. "Ah…but obviously I can," he said as he continued stroking her mind.

Shelley gulped, struggling to make sense of the sensations coursing through her body. Aching, sharp pain on one side.

Seductive pleasure on the other, she almost felt her mind shutting down, just accepting the sensations that made no sense, blending them into one blinding, overwhelmingly stunning sensation of need. Racking need clawed through her entire body. She groaned and panted, unable to focus.

"Breathe through the need," Talcor demanded.

Shelley felt a wash of cool energy soothing her. He backed off and brought the worst of the pain to a tolerable, manageable level at the same time that he blended pleasure into the mix.

She wanted to deny the control Talcor claimed. She tried to calm her racing heart, to ignore the images Talcor painted in her head. Images of her surrender. Images of his power swept her away.

"Take me," she cried, not able to prevent a slight wobble to the demand, lessening its impact.

"When I'm ready," he said, grinning mischievously, as if he knew how angry those words would make her.

She squirmed.

"You are so lovely," he murmured as he slid his hands down the sides of her chest, past her hips, down to her feet.

Then his hands moved up the inside of her legs. He spread her labia, exposing her glistening pink cunt. "You look empty," he stated, flicking a finger to stroke her clit. Shelley closed her eyes, sinking into the bed, moaning at the delicate, teasing touch. She wanted more. As if sensing her need, Talcor moved to her clit and sucked it into his mouth at the same time that he rammed his fingers deep inside her.

He moved in her head again, shoving her back from the peak.

Shelley screamed, "Stop! I can't take any more!"

Talcor ignored her demand. With one last lick, Talcor again captured her head and forced her to breathe. "I've never been able to create pain and pleasure without tools. It is a heady experience."

She swung between pleasure and pain until she couldn't separate the two and simply sank into the sensations Talcor created like a maestro playing first one instrument then another. He created a wave of pain then a wave of pleasure and even as she rode one wave, it echoed back again and again, mixing with its opposite.

"Talcor...please," she breathed out, not sure why or what she needed at this point. Her body felt more alive than she'd ever imagined it could be. She no longer knew what she needed or why. It was as if her mind had shut down as Talcor controlled her feelings. She craved his domination and control. He'd take care of her. He'd tell her what must be done. She no longer had to worry or plan or struggle.

He laughed. "How do you feel about my games now?"

Shelley struggled to form a coherent answer.

She felt herself as if from a distance. Her nerve endings were tight with need. She couldn't determine if it was a need for pain or a need for pleasure. The two blended into a mixture of want and she realized that she longed to beg for more. No man had ever sent her to the places Talcor was showing her.

She rode the pain, feeling euphoric, and she moaned when he moved away. The lassitude flooded her body, making her forget that Talcor might not be done with her.

It was a shock when she felt something against her anus. Talcor still lay on top of her, his hands on her face. There was no object at her anus, only Talcor controlling her sensations.

"No," she moaned, frightened by the helplessness of her position as she felt a cold pressure below. The object was slimy, as if coated with some kind of jelly.

"Just accept the sensation — don't fight it," he murmured.

Shelley swallowed hard, coming out of her dreamy state to say, "Please, Talcor..."

He paused. "Please what?"

She didn't answer.

"Please stop? Please do more? Please no more pain? Please more pain? What do you want, Shelley? Tell me," Talcor demanded.

Tears misted her eyes. "I don't know!"

"Do you trust me, Shelley?"

She wanted to scream at him. She wanted to tell him that no, of course she didn't trust him but she couldn't because, somehow she did trust him. No man had ever played her body the way he did and she was rapidly becoming addicted to the glorious sensations he caused. The pain, the pleasure all mixed together into a sensual blend that overwhelmed all her common sense and swept her away into a world she'd never imagined. She closed her eyes and nodded.

"Then say it," he said.

She opened her eyes and met his demanding stare, briefly wondering what would happen if she denied her trust of him. His implacable face seemed to dare her to defy him. She took in a deep breath, and said, "I trust you."

He smiled and mentally pushed the object deep into her rectum, tearing a scream from her throat as his weight prevented her from moving away from the imaginary object. Before she could adjust, Talcor created other toys, shoving something large into her cunt and attaching a clamp to her clit.

The resulting sensations overwhelmed her nervous system. Shaking, she screamed, trying to squirm away while firmly held in place, throbbing and aching. Sharp, shooting pains blended while Talcor continued to hold her head and gently but firmly kiss her, robbing her of breath until she almost passed out.

When she struggled back to awareness, the objects were gone. Talcor held her chin in one hand while the other toyed with her nipple. Her body ached as if she'd had real sex, not a mental exercise.

"I'm sorry. I don't have a level on my powers over you. I didn't mean to push so far," he said.

"I still haven't had an orgasm," she replied.

He smiled. "Well, we'll have to fix that, won't we?" He gave her a soft kiss before shifting his pelvis.

Shelley stilled as she felt the head of his cock at her entrance. He pushed a little and Shelley's outer lips stretched to take him. She felt the air against her clitoris and knew that even one touch would send her over the edge of the cliff he'd led her to. She whimpered, wanting that touch, but he held her tightly as he slowly pushed forward. He rocked back and forth, accustoming her to his size. Her muscles clenched, trying to hold him, but he was stronger and he took his time — never rushing, never satisfying her and never giving her enough.

Sweat glistened on their bodies. He pushed forward again. This time though, he didn't stop, he didn't hesitate. Shelley lost herself in the feeling of Talcor filling her. His hips pushed forward and his cock split her pussy wider than it had ever been. He filled her so full that she imagined she felt him in her throat.

Shelley groaned. His cock filled her but she knew she hadn't taken him all.

"You will take all of me," Talcor whispered, and Shelley felt a thrill of fear and excitement at his promise. She strained against her bonds, her collar firm against her throat.

He rocked back and forth a little, each time going a millimeter deeper, each time expanding her a little more, fighting for room. Shelley's pussy burned, yet she moved to meet Talcor's strokes, mistaking the pain for pleasure. Talcor reached down and lifted Shelley's buttocks, forcing her pelvis up so he could fully sink himself within her warmth.

Her eyes widened and she saw a gleam of satisfaction race through his eyes. She heard him in her mind, *Say the following, out loud — I am Talcor's companion and we are bound forever — physically, mentally and spiritually.*

"I..." She started to say, but her voice broke. Swallowing past the lump in her still-sore throat, she tried again, "I am Talcor's companion and we are bound forever—physically, mentally and spiritually." She spoke softly but her voice echoed in the stone room.

Talcor's voice rang out as he said, "We are bonded companions. We are one body, one mind, one spirit."

He ground his pelvis against her clitoris and Shelley moaned as every muscle in her body tensed. But the pressure didn't hang on the peak this time. A scream ripped from her throat as deep within a band of pressure exploded, clenching and releasing around Talcor's buried cock.

She felt his throbbing, hot stream of semen an instant before Talcor's climax exploded in her mind. As if they were one person, his pleasure became hers. She felt the jetting spurts leave his body. She felt her vagina tight and cling, sucking every ounce from his body. She felt his energies burrow into every fiber of her being. She felt his release, so long withheld, multiply and echo deep within. Her release continued for a long time until blinding satisfaction flooded every part of Shelley's body.

Talcor kept a hand on her shoulder, his forehead touching hers and she closed her eyes. Feeling battered and bewildered, she gladly accepted his touch, too confused to move. She wanted to enjoy the feeling of joy that suffused her.

She would never have to say no again. She'd never be alone again. Peace flooded and calmed her exhausted body. Confident that Talcor would keep her safe, she fell into a light sleep.

Shelley lost track of time. Every time she woke, Talcor took her again.

* * * * *

Until one morning she awoke alone. The restraints had been removed. Where was Talcor? Even as she thought of him, the door opened and he entered the bedroom.

Shelley's cunt clenched at the sight of him. He moved to the bed and bent to capture her lips, the kiss hard and deep. Shelley wound her arms around his neck and pulled him on top of her. His weight a comfort, promising safety.

He pulled back and looked down at her, "We've been here long enough. Shower, get dressed then come downstairs," he said before turning and leaving the bedroom.

Shelley struggled to organize her thoughts. How long had they been isolated in the bedroom? At least a week, probably more. She'd lost all track of time she realized. Sighing, she slowly crawled out of bed, her body aching but content. The shower helped her focus and as she made her way downstairs, she wondered what Talcor planned now.

Pella and Jared sat in the dining room. They smiled up at her.

A twinge of embarrassment flitted through Shelley until she noticed Pella's collar.

"You're bonded?"

"As are you," Jared replied.

Shelley smiled ruefully. "I guess I am at that." She helped herself to food. She'd just finished eating when Talcor entered the room.

"Come," he said. "I have a surprise for you."

"What?"

"You'll see," he replied, holding out his hand.

Shelley stood and took his hand.

He led her to his air car. After a short time, he circled a large castle-like structure. Talcor landed and helped Shelley from the air car. "Come on."

She held back a little, wondering what could excite him so much.

"Normally, as a newly bound couple, we would still be in isolation. Davo has been acting as our watcher." Talcor paused and met her eyes. "Kytar will take over now."

"Kytar..." Shelley trailed off. "That means..."

"Yes," he smiled. Tugging on her hand, he led her to the door.

It flew open and a petite woman with long blonde hair ran toward Shelley.

"Marissa!" Shelley exclaimed, exchanging a big hug with the other woman. "You look..."

"I'm sure I look well, content and satisfied." Marissa paused, cocked her head and said, "As do you, Shelley."

"You're happy?" Shelley asked.

"Very happy."

"What have these men done to you?"

"Kytar has taught me things about myself that I never knew. Shelley, I'm happy. You don't have to worry about me."

"But that vid I saw?"

"I heard you saw it but you only saw a small part. You didn't see the entire thing. Shelley, I'm happy and thrilled that you're here too."

A large man moved close to Marissa. "It is time," he said, smiling down at her.

"I'm going to miss this place," Marissa said. Then she turned to Shelley and gave her a big hug. "It's your turn to enjoy its isolation." She smiled and turned to Kytar. Linking arms, they moved to the air car. Marissa turned and waved before they climbed inside.

Shelley and Talcor watched them get settled and take off.

"Come. Let me show you my ancestral home and some of the very special toys it contains," Talcor said as he grabbed Shelley's hand and led her inside.

Also by Cyna Kade

ɞ

eBooks:

Linking Shelley

Mastering Marissa

Power and Pain 1: Releasing Kate

Power and Pain 2: Outside Sanctuary

Power and Pain 3: Inside Sanctuary

Stripped by Love

Tamara's Future

Tessa's Ambassador

Print Books:

Mastering Marissa

Pirate's Prisoner *(anthology)*

Power and Pain 1: Releasing Kate

About the Author

ò

Cyna Kade started reading science fiction and fantasy when she was ten. By age fifteen, she added romance to her reading list. Erotica followed much later. Cyna believes the best books mix genres and she's followed that belief in her life. She's lived in north, east, south and west. She's been married and liberated and deeply loves her children. She's worked as an x-ray tech, a computer programmer, a systems analyst, a university instructor and earned a multidisciplinary Ph.D. Hobbies are equally varied, including stained glass and tai chi.

ò

The author welcomes comments from readers. You can find her website and email address on her author bio page at www.ellorascave.com.

Tell Us What You Think

We appreciate hearing reader opinions about our books. You can email us at Comments@EllorasCave.com.

Why an electronic book?

We live in the Information Age—an exciting time in the history of human civilization, in which technology rules supreme and continues to progress in leaps and bounds every minute of every day. For a multitude of reasons, more and more avid literary fans are opting to purchase e-books instead of paper books. The question from those not yet initiated into the world of electronic reading is simply: *Why?*

1. *Price.* An electronic title at Ellora's Cave Publishing runs anywhere from 40% to 75% less than the cover price of the exact same title in paperback format. Why? Basic mathematics and cost. It is less expensive to publish an e-book (no paper and printing, no warehousing and shipping) than it is to publish a paperback, so the savings are passed along to the consumer.

2. *Space.* Running out of room in your house for your books? That is one worry you will never have with electronic books. For a low one-time cost, you can purchase a handheld device specifically designed for e-reading. Many e-readers have large, convenient screens for viewing. Better yet, hundreds of titles can be stored within your new library—on a single microchip. There are a variety of e-readers from different manufacturers. You can also read e-books on your PC or laptop computer. (Please note that Ellora's Cave does not endorse any specific brands.

You can check our website at www.ellorascave.com for information we make available to new consumers.)

3. *Mobility.* Because your new e-library consists of only a microchip within a small, easily transportable e-reader, your entire cache of books can be taken with you wherever you go.

4. *Personal Viewing Preferences.* Are the words you are currently reading too small? Too large? Too... ANNOYING? Paperback books cannot be modified according to personal preferences, but e-books can.

5. *Instant Gratification.* Is it the middle of the night and all the bookstores near you are closed? Are you tired of waiting days, sometimes weeks, for bookstores to ship the novels you bought? Ellora's Cave Publishing sells instantaneous downloads twenty-four hours a day, seven days a week, every day of the year. Our webstore is never closed. Our e-book delivery system is 100% automated, meaning your order is filled as soon as you pay for it.

Those are a few of the top reasons why electronic books are replacing paperbacks for many avid readers.

As always, Ellora's Cave welcomes your questions and comments. We invite you to email us at Comments@ellorascave.com or write to us directly at Ellora's Cave Publishing Inc., 1056 Home Avenue, Akron, OH 44310-3502.

ELLORA'S CAVE
Romanticon

Annual convention
for women who
refuse to behave

Discover for yourself why readers can't get enough
of the multiple award-winning publisher

Ellora's Cave.

Whether you prefer e-books or paperbacks,

be sure to visit EC on the web at
www.ellorascave.com

for an erotic reading experience that will leave you
breathless.

CPSIA information can be obtained at www.ICGtesting.com
Printed in the USA
LVOW060902290412

279558LV00001B/56/P